Snow

B.K. Leigh

COPYRIGHT

DEDICATION

For my loves, Cameron and Birdie.

Snow

Chapter 1

Adeline

I latch onto Jaimie's hand tighter as we weave our way through the thick throngs of students from our graduate class. Usually these parties seem much smaller, but tonight it's as if every single student from Mount Claire High is jam packed into Tim Singers tiny two story house. The loud bass vibrates off the walls and pounds against my ear drums the deeper we go. The smiling faces of all the kids we graduated with only hours ago surround us completely. Down the hall and to the left we would have made it to our destination, but as we pass by the packed kitchen, I tug on Jaimie's hand and pull him in behind me.

My eyes roam around the littered countertops until they find exactly what I came in search of. A handle of Jack sits perfectly untouched in the back of what must be thirty other bottles of liquor.

"Take it to go." Jaimie comes up behind me as I grab for a red solo cup. His hands come up to my waist and gently turn my body back towards him, bottle in hand. "Come on Addy, Jake and Tim are waiting for us." his lips come down to mine for a brief moment just before he turns away dragging me behind him. For a minute I almost decide against the alcohol, knowing I could get tipsy off of Jaimie himself but I know better. I don't want to be tipsy I want to be gone to the world as soon as possible and Jaimie knows it.

My eyes roam up and down Jaimie's colossal form as we make our way out to the deck. His broad shoulders ram into almost everyone we pass by and no one seems to give a damn. He's big for being just eighteen, much bigger than the other boys we just graduated with and most adults I've seen around. He's going to make a killer linebacker once he goes off to college. A sharp pain starts in my chest at the mere

2

Snow

thought of him leaving me behind with his departure
date just two short months away. In the end I know it's
inevitable. So for now I hold on just a little bit tighter.

"There he is! The future of Alabama football
himself!" Tim's loud voice brings me out of my thoughts
as we finally step out of the crowded house and out
onto the large deck. Like every other weekend Jaimie
and I take our seats around the small glass table, as Jake
and Tim pass a joint back and forth. I met Tim and Jamie
our freshman year of high school.

*Sporting a very pretty black eye for my first day
of the new school year, compliments of my mother's
most recent boyfriend, I decide to make my way out to
the football field during lunch hours. The underside of
the bleachers proved to be a good hiding spot for
someone needing to desperately get away from the
prying eyes of teachers and snide remarks of the pretty
popular girls littering the hallway. The sweet aroma of
marijuana seemed to carry me deeper and deeper
behind the metal bleachers. I wondered who else could
be out here as my feet encouraged me to move forward.
They carried me on their own accord. Soon enough I was*

3

rounding a corner only to find two troublesome looking boys passing a blunt back and forth.

"What the hell happened to your face?" the skinny redhead on the left nearly coughs up a lung when he takes in my appearance. The much larger boy on the right only seems to penetrate me with his piercing blue eyes. Both seem to have an incredibly annoying staring problem.

"What's it to you?" I ask as I stick a hand out. Their eyes widen. "Well are you going to share or what?" I wait impatiently for the redhead to make up his mind before he cautiously hands over the small rolled joint. I bring the joint to my lips and listen as the redhead begins to speak again.

"I'm Tim, and this is Jaimie." He points to the boy beside him and I nod. A mop of shaggy brown hair and piercing blue eyes stare at me like I'm some sort of circus freak. His stare is curious, and searching for something I don't think he'll find.

"Addy." I reply handing the joint back over. "So, are you going to be here tomorrow?"

Snow

That was that. The beginning of the end. At least for us. From then on it was the three of us. Where I went they followed, and the other way around. As the years passed on Jaimie, Tim and I seemed to uphold a pretty solid do-not-fuck-with-us reputation. No one messed with us or even tried to befriend us. It was only in junior year when we added another body to our pack, Jake. He was just like us, so it was easy for him to make himself at home. The four of us were misfits, all seeming to come from some form of fucked up home life to the other. The circumstances were unfortunate, but our bond seemed unbreakable. Jaimie and I grew closer. Our bond seemed to be soul deep. We were best friends, but sometimes it was more than that. We cuddled, kissed and held hands, but never crossed over that invisible line. It was like an unspoken agreement, and one I was perfectly fine with. Tim and Jake both knew what Jaimie and I did behind closed doors. After a while it wasn't long before other people started to assume things. We never corrected them.

"Here." My eyes focus back on the three boys and I watch as Tim hands Jake the joint. My hands itch

5

to grab it and have it all to myself but I wait for my turn like the good girl I am.

"Gimme, gimme!" I finally reach for the blunt and inhale as soon as the sweet taste of bubble gum kush hits my lips. I feel the slow burn of the smoke all the way into my lungs and relish when I feel the fog start to cloud my mind. Hit after hit, I stay in my own little bubble as the three boys chat nonstop around me with the soft thump of the bass pounding in the background. I'm finally at peace. Finally I can breathe again.

"Damn Addy you're going hard tonight." Jake's rough voice speaks up as I pull the blunt from my lips only to replace it with the neck of the Jack Daniels bottle.

"Yeah, well it's been a rough few days." I hand it over to Jaimie, and watch as his soft lips close around what's left of the joint, inhaling just as deeply as I did. His piercing blue eyes stare deep into my soul as I become completely lost in him. I stand up from my chair and make my way into his lap and relax completely when his large arms wrap tightly around my torso. I let

Snow

the haze slowly take over my body. Head to toe. The
lightweight feeling is what I crave. One by one all
thoughts seem to drain from my brain as my body
suddenly becomes free. Light as a feather, free as a
bird.

A loud bang sounds from next door, causing me
to jump. In the dark of the night I can make out the size
of a monstrous man. His shadow alone seems to tower
over the wooden fence and creep into the backyard of
Tim's house.

"There he is!" Tim whisper shouts to the group.
Jaimie's hand slides under my sweatshirt as all of the
attention is placed on the recluse next door. "That's
Gideon Wellfleet." Tim states. I've heard his name in
whispers by the town folk, a young veteran whose mind
is crippled by the war. He ended up in Brookfield by
chance. While he was away a freak car accident claimed
both of his parents, and now he resides in what used to
be their home. Some people say he's all sorts of fucked
up. The trauma of the war seemed to be eating away at
his mind until he went completely bat shit crazy and

7

killed a guy... At least that's what Sharon at the liquor store said.

"Didn't he just get back from overseas?" Jake asks. "I heard he killed some sort of Jehovah's Witness guy who walked up to his door." See, I told you.

"That's not true Jake, you can't believe everything people say. "I comment before taking another swig from the bottle. Jaimie's hand caresses my stomach in small circles as I lean back into him. All the while my eyes remain on the mysterious man dragging two huge black trash bags slowly behind him.

"Yeah well they said your mom is a crack whore and you're her crack addicted baby and that turned out to be true." He shrugs his shoulders as if he didn't just insult me.

"Hey fuck you Jake!" I throw the empty bottle towards his head but he ducks just before it makes contact with the deck and completely shatters. The commotion causes the mystery guy to turn his attention toward us and for a moment I'm stunned. Thirty feet separate him from us and yet I feel the piercing stare of his cold eyes as they bore into mine. My body stills, only the feel of Jaimie's rhythmic hand keeps me grounded.

"Fuck Jake, he fucking heard you." Tim ducks as if that's going to conceal him from his neighbor. The high from the weed must be fucking with his mind if he thinks he's been unseen.

"Tim, he's thirty feet away he can see and hear almost everything you say and do." Jake gestures towards the group of us and raging party going on inside. "Speaking of, maybe you should go check on things." As soon as the words leave his mouth the sound of glass shattering has our heads turning toward the house.

"Oh for fucks sake, this is why I didn't want all these goddamn people here." Tim stands up and starts walking towards the sound of the commotion. When I turn my attention back to the man next door he's gone. All the lights in his completely out, doors and windows locked tight.

"That better not have been my mom's china, or so help me god." Tim warns as he stalks inside, his bright red hair drifting like flames in the wind.

B.K. Leigh

"I should go help him." Jake makes a beeline after Tim and suddenly Jaimie and I are completely alone.

"Mmm, you feel good." I lay my head back against him, and let my alcohol soaked mind close off almost completely. My skin feels tingly. The feel of Jaimie's fingertips running up and down my arms has my body on fire.

"Stop squirming Addy." His arms lock tight around me holding me securely in place.

"Why Jaimie? Does it feel good?" I tease. I turn my eyes on him and get caught on the other end of his heated gaze.

"You know what you do to me Addy." Suddenly I'm turned in his lap, straddling his hips with my thighs. His lips are on mine in an instant. His hardness pressed up against my core, begging for more connection. Our mouths mold into one while our tongues explore the others. I never get tired of his lips against mine. Although it doesn't feel romantic in any way it feels more comforting, like it's the most normal thing in the entire world. Our connection is soul deep, best friends

10

to the depths of our core. It sounds ridiculous, but the kind of love we share is not the kind of a couple 'in love'. My hands wrap around his neck, and I bask in the warmth his body brings mine.

"Don't leave me Jaimie, I need you." I whisper against his lips. I unleash my deepest secret of despair, the alcohol making me feel more brave than normal.

"It's not for good Addy, you know that." His lips nibble against mine. "I'll be back before you know it, you'll survive." I bury myself further against him and hang on tight. Afraid to let him go.

"I won't, I know it." I reply.

"You'll have Tim and Jake. They won't let anything happen to you. You know that." He tries to bargain with me, but it's not the same. My mind is made up.

"But they're not you." He rubs his fingers gently through my hair, and my eyelids droop closed. The burn of alcohol flows steadily through my blood turning my limbs heavy, and threatening to close my mind off completely.

"Shhh... Just close your eyes baby, it's going to be alright." I do what he says enjoying the feel of his body against mine. I sigh in relief. "Come on Addy let's get your drunk ass home." I feel his weight shift from under me as he stands. Finally only in the comfort of his arms, the darkness takes over and I'm finally at peace.

*****

I wake the next morning with a pounding headache. The small sliver of sunlight peeking through the shades has my eyes squinting and my stomach churning. I roll onto my side ready to wake Jaimie up after a long night of partying but the spot where I usually find him is empty. A glass of water, bottle of ibuprofen, and small white piece of paper sit on top of the small bedside table. I reach for the pills and water first and probably down more than I should take. The cool taste of the water sliding down my throat begins to wash away the remnants of the marijuana smoke from last night. I force myself into a sitting position and grab for the little note Jaimie left me. Why wouldn't he have just texted me?

Snow

Addy, baby

For starters, here's some water and ibuprofen. After last night you're probably going to need it. Try not to take too much. By the time you've woken up, I'll be halfway to Alabama. When I told you I'd be going to ASU I never mentioned I'd be leaving for the summer football program. I knew if I had told you sooner it'd be all you could think about, and our last few weeks together wouldn't have been like they were. Tim and Jake will take care of you, nothing has to change baby. I'll be back before you know it, but while I'm gone I want you to live your life. Take chances and fall in love, hell... find a new best friend. Wipe the tears away and get the fuck out of that place you call home. Do something big for me Addy. And please don't beat up the guy's, I made them keep their mouths shut. I love you always Addy baby.

Your best friend, Jaimie

The further I read the more my face falls and my heart sinks. By the end I'm raging mad. I wipe away the stray tears and crumple up the flimsy piece of paper. *He fucking left me?* I grab for my phone and

13

immediately dial his number, patiently waiting for his answer. Hoping this was all some joke, that the shitty crumpled piece of paper thrown across my bedroom floor is just a sick fucking joke. *How could he?* Over and over again my calls continue to go unanswered only heightening my blinding rage. I start to pace around my small bedroom floor, tears threaten to come flowing out like a damn ready to burst, but I won't let that happen.

I throw on the nearest T-shirt and grab a hair tie off the bedside table to tie my wayward curls back. Fuck taking a shower, that can wait. I peek my head outside my bedroom door and listen. Nothing but silence fills the air. The stench of cigarette smoke and putrid body odor wafts through the small opened crack in the door wrapping around me like a strait jacket, threatening to send all the contents of my stomach up in one blow. Tip toeing through the hall I step over my mother's limp body and sneak past the fat burly man asleep on the sofa. I escape out the front door unseen and unnoticed. Five minutes later I arrive at my destination fuming and ready to kick some fucking ass.

Snow

Bang! Bang! Bang!

I stare at the sliding glass door as I wait for someone to answer. My fists are unrelenting, I know they're in there, probably still fucked up from the night before.

Bang! Bang! Bang!

I pound again and take in the ruins of what used to be Tim's perfectly manicured lawn all around me. Beer bottles and cans are strewn here and there, with other pieces of trash covering almost every inch off grass. Chairs and other pieces of furniture are thrown in the pool, helplessly floating around the green tinted water.

"Alright, alright! Hold your horses. I'm fucking coming!" Jake's sleepy form appears on the other side of the glass door. His hair is tasseled, and the bags under his eyes seem to have grown tenfold over the past night. I guess we all had one hell of a time. He takes in my disheveled appearance and cautiously opens the door.

"Addy what the hell are you doing here? What time is it?" he runs a tired hand through his messy hair and steps out onto the deck entering my space. In one swift motion I swing my hand back fast bringing it forward right across his cheek. My breathing is hard and heavy. The sting of the pain spreads across my hand much like the angry red heat spreading across Jake's sensitive skin.

"Jesus fucking Christ, Adeline. What the hell was that for?" He yells as he cradles his cheek with his hand.

"You fucking know what that was for Jake, he fucking left!" I scream in his face. Once again the angry tears threaten to fall down my hot cheeks. "You knew he was leaving and didn't even tell me!" my chest heaves up and down as the impact of my words dawn on him.

"What the hell is going on out here?" Tim stumbles out onto the deck in just a pair of basketball shorts. His red hair shines like fire in the morning sunlight. Before he even gets the chance to defend himself my palm connects with the right side of his face, leaving him with an identical angry red mark as Jake. "What the hell was that for Addy?" his head swings

16

back and forth between Jake and I searching for
answers.

"You guys knew Jaimie was leaving the whole
fucking time, and didn't even have the guts to tell me?"
my voice comes out in a high pitched shrill. I watch as
Tim throws his hands over his ears to block out the
horrible sound. I sound like a rabid animal, but honestly
it's not much far from how I feel inside.

"Jesus fucking Christ, Addy. What do want us to
do? He didn't want us to say anything to you!" Jake's
voice rolls from his mouth like thunder in a storm, and I
know right away he's on the edge.

"You guys are supposed to be my friends!" I
shout at the top of my lungs. Hurt clings on to each
word that spews from my mouth. "You guys fucking
lied, for days you all fucking knew and didn't tell me."
The look on their faces tells me they don't understand
where I'm coming from and it only causes my heart to
crack further. How could they not know? How could
they possibly not know Jaimie was my savior, my best
friend and confident. They were there every day, every
time I came to Jaimie upset, broken and bruised. They

17

saw the connection, how could the three of them just assume I'd be okay with this? Did they really think I wouldn't have an absolute fucking breakdown?

"I'm sorry, Add's. Jaimie will be back in a few months. It's not forever." But he just doesn't understand. I need Jaimie like a little kid needs his favorite blanket or a night light. I need him to protect me from all the dark and scary things I have to face in life, and now he's not here. I have to face everything alone.

My legs almost buckle as I place my hands on my knees, trying to keep in my nearing melt down.

"Oh fuck. Fuck, fuck, fuck, fuck." I whisper yell to myself. Everything's suddenly all too much. The pressure pressing down on my shoulders threatens to suffocate me with every breath I take.

"Fuck, Add's. Are you okay?" I hear Tim's muffled voice break through the ringing in my ears.

"What the fuck is wrong with her? Addy you okay?" Jake's head turns to Tim then me, and just as I look up red spots start to blur my vision. It's been forever since I had an anxiety attack. The last time

Snow

Jaimie was the only one who managed to get me to calm the fuck down.

"I need something." My throat cracks as I force the words out. "Anything… Jack, weed please just give me something and get me it quick." The words crumbling from my lips sound exactly like the woman I despise most in the world… my mother. I hate that I've become her, I hate that I need drugs or alcohol to calm me, to fix me, to make me feel normal again. I hear shuffling on the deck and seconds later Tim slams a half empty bottle of Tequila in my hands. I smash it against my lips in a matter of seconds. I gulp and gulp until the burning in my throat finally calms my boiling blood, and levels my raging thoughts. I chug until I can clearly see through to the bottom. I chug until the heavy weight of the bottle feels next to nothing. I chug until the bottle's empty and my legs are numb. Ten o'clock in the morning and I'm already completely wasted. Tim and Jake watch me in shock or disbelief. At this point I'm not sure which is which.

"Addy, you might wanna slow down a little, you don't look okay…" Jake's voice trails off as I drop the bottle to the ground and try to focus my eyes on him. I guess you could say I'm a lightweight or maybe I just drank the bottle way too fast on an already hungover and empty stomach. The alcohol has already taken affect over my whole entire body. Besides my mom always says the best cure for a hangover is more booze. I take a seat in my usual chair and ignore the pain it causes me when I look to Jaimie's empty one.

"Fuck," Tim swears, brushing the flames of hair out of his face. He's swaying from foot to foot, or maybe that's just me? I don't know at this point. My brain feels fuzzy and my blood feels warm. "If you can't beat em' join em'." He finishes. His body takes up residence across from me and I watch as he fishes a rolled joint out of his shorts pocket. The cherry burns bright red as he breathes in the smoke and my heart drums in anticipation. For now I'm good. I can forget about Jaimie, at least for a few hours...minutes...seconds? I don't really know anymore.

"Shit, this is going to be a long fucking day." Jake sits down finally and takes the joint from Tim. He's completely fucking right; it's going to be one long

Snow

fucking day.

Chapter 2

Gideon

Will the noise ever fucking stop? The one thing I never missed while I was away was the constant fucking noise from next door. How can someone be awake all fucking hours of the night? The house next door was constantly roaring with life no matter what time it was, no matter who they were fucking disturbing with the loud music and screams. Last night was no different than every other weekend night since I've been home. The music started early, the screams and laughter came next, the thick clouds of smoke came last and if you tried hard, the putrid stench of alcohol wafted through the air.

Snow

I finished with the meat cuts early and had to bring the trash out. I should have known there'd be a group of them sitting on the back deck, like always. The same four people grouped together away from the other party goers. Not the cause of the screams and laughter, but definitely the smoke and stench. The redhead lives there and unlike him his parents are respectful, unless they are away which is usually nine times out of ten.

Always on the redhead's left is the smaller guy out of the bunch. Scraggly brown hair and long scrawny arms. He's quiet and calculating, always hanging on to the words spread around him. Then there is the girl. Her hair is crazy curly, her skin white as a ghost. Her stare is daunting, and in the daylight I can see the haunted look in her eyes. She was always between scrawny and the beast, either that or in his lap completely. He was the biggest teenager I'd seen in a while. Bigger than some of the men I served with in Iraq. I watched them like I was trained to do, always taking in my surroundings, being ready for the fight. The fight that still raged a war inside my head.

23

B.K. Leigh

I heard the whispers as soon as my door opened. I felt her stare against my back as I made my way to the trash bins. *He's a murderer. He's weird. He's a recluse.* All things I've been used to since my return. They're right; I'm all of those things. I am a murderer, but not in the way they've been told. I am weird, and I am a recluse. They think my minds been clouded by the war but it's far from it. I'm not crippled by the things I saw, I'm stronger, but no one else will ever know it. They see what they want to see and nothing else.

I live by myself in solidarity, and I like it that way. I leave my house only when needed, and in all reality that doesn't equal out to much. My basement is my gym, the TV feeds me my news, and once a month I manage to make it to the twenty four hour Walmart right here in town. There are less people at two o'clock in the morning. The rumors stick to a low, and I can shop my way through the store without all of the penetrating eyes and hushed whispers.

When I saw the girl get carried away by the beast I thought it was finally over. The music died down and people started filing out of the house in succession.

24

Snow

It was quiet for what seemed like a few hours, and for once in a long time I managed to actually shut my goddamn eyes.

Bang! Bang! Bang!

My eyes fly open as my heart starts pounding. My hand instantly grabs for the gun on my bedside table, ready to spring into action.

Bang! Bang! Bang!

I drop to the floor and crawl over to the window military style. My eyes lift just enough above the wooden plank to give me visual on the outside. My heart rate slows down and I raise myself up into a standing position as my eyes laid sight on the girl next door. It's just her. She looks angry, livid, but poses no immediate threat of danger. I put the gun back in its usual spot and continue to watch out the window. *Okay, so maybe I'm a tad bit fucked up.*

I watch as the scrawny guy answers the door and she belts him hard across the face. Her voice only seems to get louder and louder. I crack the window open just a little to try and get a better listen.

B.K. Leigh

"Jesus fucking Christ, Adeline. What the hell was that for!" the scrawny guy yells, holding onto his bright red cheek. Addy, Adeline, her name is beautiful. It's not the first time I've heard it, read about it, or wrote it down in a series of notes.

The redhead steps out next and suffers the same fate as the first boy. Adeline packs a mean punch. I watch in awe as they yell back and forth, until finally she almost doubles over in pain. My heart lurches as I watch her try to catch her breath. My feet itch to move in her direction. The medic within me wanted to help in a time of need as I watched her body crumple over, and fold in pain. I knew she was having some sort of panic attack. The redhead runs inside in a panic and comes outside thrusting a bottle of clear liquid into her waiting palms. Her head tips back and for a fraction of a second I manage to see the brokenness eating at her soul inside. She chugs the liquid until its empty, until she's swaying back and forth on her feet. No doubt the alcohol has already taken effect on her tiny frame.

I watch until she finally sits down, and the two guys follow in suit. I watch for seconds, minutes and

26

hours. She stays in the same spot, almost all day. The two boys next to her moving around every once in a while, shifting from inside the house and out. They supply her with more drinks, hand her more joints, and watch as she slowly fades into a stupor. Hours later her head falls back and the shallow breaths floating through her lungs have her chest rising and falling at an incredibly slow pace. The redhead and scrawny boy retired hours ago leaving her to sleep all alone on the back deck, only returning at dusk to drape a thin blanket across her shoulders.

My body feels stiff as I finally force myself to leave and cook myself dinner. I step into the kitchen with Adeline at the back of my mind, and come face to face with Max's frowning face.

"I'm sorry boy, I didn't forget about you." I lean over to pet his head as he lays unamused at my feet. "I'll get your dinner started boy." At this I swear I get an eye roll. Max was my inherited dog from my parents. Max their precious St. Bernard came along with the house in the will. I swear all he does is eat and sleep. Getting him to go outside is an actual struggle and in a way he seems to be exactly like me. He's a recluse in his own sense, maybe that's why we get along so well or maybe it's just the fact that I give him his dinner every night and an extra piece of steak for dessert. About an hour later I take a seat at the dining room table and take a bite of my steak and potatoes. Max eats quietly on the floor beside me.

I check the time and realize it's already ten o'clock. I look around and bask in the silence. Its ten o'clock at night and house beside mine is completely silent. I finish my meal and bringing the empty dishes to the sink. Wrapping up the trash I pace by the kitchen window and notice Adeline is no longer outside... finally. She must have gone inside after sleeping the whole entire day off. I open the door with Max hot on my heels and take the short walk out to the trash bins. I hear a short bark and watch as Max's huge furry body runs off to the front yard. "Max! Hey!" I call after him. I'm confused when he doesn't come trotting back to me.

"Max, Come here boy!" I let out a whistle and walk my way around the side of the house. In the

Snow

darkness I see his body in the middle of the yard.
"Max!" I call again but he doesn't budge. He lets out a
short bark and stays put. The closer I get the more I
begin to see the picture in front of me. Max is hovering
over a body. It's not just any body, it's Adeline. My legs
move at record speed. I land on my knees right beside
her, immediately checking for a pulse. She's still
breathing, but it's immensely shallow.

I scoop her up in my arms and carry her inside,
Max hot on my tail. I manage to get the door shut and
locked behind me as I weave my way through the house
to the back bedroom on the left. I place her on the bed
and take in her appearance. Her sweat soaked hair is
sticking to her pale forehead. The T-shirt covering her
small frame has what seems to be throw up splashed
across the front of it. Grass stains mar her knees and
palms, and black mascara runs in streaks down her
cheeks. Max hovers over her like a bodyguard as I try to
pry the sweaty clothes from her body and get her
changed into something new. I grab an old T-shirt from
my drawer and attempt to put it on her. Her body is
limp mostly, but every once in a while she wakes.

"Jaimie?" she whispers. Her voice is low, almost childlike. I lay her backward and cover her body with a clean sheet. Her body looks frail and fragile in the middle of my large king sized bed. Max jumps up to lay beside her and I instantly scold him.

"Max! No, you know you're not allowed on the furniture!" I talk to him like he's a child, like he can understand me. The way he looks back at me tells me he does but is unbothered by it. I attempt to move his huge massive body, but he nips at my hand, moving closer towards Adeline. In her sleep she turns on her side, her tiny hand embedding itself deep in Max's long fur. Hmph. I guess it's decided then. "Fine boy, you win. But only for tonight." He rolls his eyes and takes up residence in the spot closest to Adeline for the night. Fucking dog.

I grab a free pillow off the bed and make my journey to the living room. It's ironic, it's my house and yet I'm the one having to sleep on the couch. It feels like hours have gone by with the darkness and silence surrounding me completely. My thoughts are consumed with the girl sleeping in the room just down the hall. I can't help but wonder what the cause of her pain is. Why she could just sit outside for hours and drink herself into a stupor. How messed up could someone seriously be to drink their lives away? She seems so young to already be addicted to drugs and alcohol but I guess this day and age anything is possible. Knowing who her mother is, things slowly begin to make sense.

And who is Jaimie? She spoke his name more than once when I was in the room with her. My thoughts run rampant in for hours on end until finally my body tires out and my eyes become sleepy. The thought of a sleeping Adeline in my house still resides in the back of my mind. The last thought I have before sleep finally takes over is that it's going to be a long fucking night, a very long fucking night.

*****

I wake the next morning to the sound of the bathroom door shutting. The switch of the lock on the inside echoes down the hall. I reach for my gun and come up empty handed then realize I'm still on the couch. There's not an intruder in the bathroom, it's just the girl from last night... Adeline. I wait in silence for her

31

to finish and make her way back into the bedroom, no doubt confused as to how she got there. The sound of my feet padding down the hallway is the only sound in the entire house. I come to a standstill in the middle of the bedroom door frame. Adeline sits cross legged on the bed, Max's head draped in her lap. The two little white pills and glass of water I left in the night stand are gone.

"Adeline." My voice comes out gruff and catches her by surprise. Her eyes instantly snap to mine, the hand petting Max stops midway above his head. She stays frozen for what seems like forever.

"Did we…did I." her cheeks flush as she tries to continue her question. "Did we have sex?" she nearly chokes out. Her cheeks are redder than a fire engine.

"No, we did not." her shoulders slump as her small thin hand comes up to rest against her forehead.

"How did I get here?" she asks. Max lifts his head to the sound of her voice as if answering her question himself.

"I found you out in the yard." Max takes that exact moment to let out a bark and send me an angry stare. "Max found you out in the yard. I brought you inside, cleaned you up and let you sleep." I nod in Max's direction and turn back to find Adeline's eyes piercing into mine, waiting for answers.

"Did you...see me naked?" she blushes crimson red as the words rush from her round heart shaped lips.

"I only removed your dirty clothes to replace them with something clean while I washed the others. It was nothing more than that." I assure her and turn to leave.

"Wait!" she calls at my back. I come to a halt. I slowly turn around and face her small pale frame. "What's your name?" she asks me, and yet I know she already knows. The whole freaking town knows who I am.

"Gideon... Gideon Wellfleet." It takes a while for her to speak once more.

"Thank you Gideon, for helping me." she smiles, but not before long it falters. In an instant she runs past me with her hand over her mouth, spilling all of the contents in her stomach into the toilet. I wince at her retching and can remember a time or two way back when I had done the same. Maybe not to the same extent but it is all in the same. I leave her to her misery and make my way to the kitchen. At the sound of pans and pots banging around Max finally emerges from the bedroom.

"Oh so now you want to come out, huh?" I say as he makes his way over to his empty bowl. "You get to sleep in my nice clean comfortable bed all night long next to a pretty girl, and then come out here and get your food handed to you." He sighs in agreement.

"Man sometimes I wish we could trade places boy." I scramble up some eggs and bacon, while Max chows down his dog food and silently waits for me to throw him an extra slice or two. Adeline emerges into the kitchen sporting fresh clothes and a clean face. The raccoon eyes she had earlier are no longer there, only to be replaced with dark under circles. She's had a rough night but, hopefully she learned her lesson.

"Take a seat." I gesture to the empty seat at the table, but she timidly shakes her head no.

Snow

"Oh no, I can't stay." She tucks a wayward hair behind her ear. "My mom, she's probably looking for me by now. I should get going."

"You should really eat something, you might still get sick on an empty stomach, and whatever food you eat will probably soak up the rest of the alcohol in your system."

"No it's okay really. I really have to go, my mom's probably going bat shit crazy by now. Thanks for... everything." She leans down to pet Max one last time and whispers something into his smushed face. I watch as she hurriedly opens the door and makes her escape. I'm left to decipher her last words. I know a lie when I hear one.

Chapter 3

Adeline

Fuck me. Seriously though this is the first thing I thought of when I opened my eyes and saw a massive dog buried into my side. I knew I wasn't in my own bedroom, and definitely not at Tim or Jake's. The walls were a smoky gray color and matched the comforter of the king sized bed I was propped up in. A few small pieces of furniture lined the walls but for the most part the room felt empty, and barren. My head was pounding and my eyes could barely open, the morning sunlight hurt like a bitch. I moved into a sitting position and dog beside me groaned as if I was disturbing him. On the nightstand next to the bed was a glass of water

and some ibuprofen which I inhaled almost
immediately.

"Where am I boy?" I ask out loud. I swear to
god this dog literally rolled his eyes at me. The last thing
I remember was being on Tim's deck for the better part
of yesterday. I had to find some way to drown out my
sorrows. The booze and weed managed to do the job
perfectly, at least for a little while. After a while Jake
and Tim managed to get tired of my drunken rantings
and headed inside leaving me alone, cold and tired.
Looking down I noticed I had on only a man sized T-shirt
and undies underneath. What the Hell?

As quietly as possible I make my way out of the
bedroom and to the nearest bathroom. Thankfully it's
right outside the door. I take in my appearance after
finishing my business and wince at myself in the mirror.
I look terrible. I literally looked as if I was hit by a truck.
My hair is matted and stuck to my forehead. The bags
under my eyes are deep and dark, and not entirely from
the black mascara smudged all over. I tip toe my way
back into the room and frantically looking around the
room for my clothes and come up empty handed. The

room starts to spin and I have to take a minute and end up back on the bed where I started.

"Adeline." A deep masculine voice pierces the silence and causes me to jump. When I look up my heart almost stops in its tracks. The darkest pair of chocolate eyes are fixated completely on me. I let my eyes travel the length of his enormous body, from his enormous biceps to the fitted T-shirt stretched tightly over his washboard abs. His hair is jet black and tousled as if he's had a rough night of sleep. Guessing by the made up sheets on the other side of the bed, he no doubt must have slept on the couch last night. It's almost impossible to force words out of my suddenly dry mouth, but somehow I manage.

"Did we...did I?" I can feel my cheeks light up like fire. "Did we have sex?" oh fuck me, did I seriously just ask that?

"No, we did not." my lungs release the breath I didn't know I was holding.

"How did I get here?" I feel the dog shift beside me as I force myself to meet his dark penetrating eyes once again.

Snow

"I found you out in the yard." Great. I'm the
spitting image of my drugged up mother, passing out on
the neighbor's lawns. "Max found you out in the yard. I
brought you inside, cleaned you up and let you sleep."
he corrects himself when the lump of fur in my lap
rejects his first statement.

"Did you see me naked?" I slap my forehead as
soon as the words flow from my lips.

"I only removed your dirty clothes to replace
them with something clean while I washed the others. It
was nothing more than that." He turns abruptly to
leave.

"Wait!" I yell and he comes to a complete stop.
"What's your name?" I ask a question me and the entire
town already knows the answer to.

"Gideon... Gideon Wellfleet." It takes me a few
minutes until I'm able to respond. The way his name
dripped from his plump lips had my throat going dry. I
can't help the way my body seems to be reacting to his.

"Thank you Gideon, for helping Me." all at once
he leaves and I'm left almost completely alone except
for the huge fur ball half laying in my lap.

39

I had one mind fuck of a morning. Never in all my drunkenness have I ever been that obliterated. I'm seriously going to have to talk to Tim and Jake about this. They'll never believe Gideon Wellfleet came to my rescue. Matter of fact they'll probably have a coronary.

Making my escape was more awkward then our initial conversation. Gideon wanted me to stay, or at least suggested I did, and I politely turned him down. I used some lame excuse like my mom must have been worried about me, which couldn't be further from the truth. A part of me thought Gideon caught onto my lies. A spark lit up in his eyes every time I tried to lie my way out of his house. He knew... he had to have. I continued my walk of shame down his driveway and all the way back to the tiny little shack I call home.

"Where've you been Addy? I'm out of cigarettes." My mother's rough smokers voice cuts through the stale air like a knife.

"I was out with Jaimie." I lie. "I'll add it to the list and grab some tonight." I trudge by her frail form stuck on the living room couch, and find my way into my bedroom. I head straight over to the top drawer of my dresser to take out the long grocery list and add on my mother's request. You know... necessities. My hand dives down deep under all the socks and underwear searching for the wad of grocery money I stashed away only to come up empty handed. My heart sinks as I start ripping all the contents of the drawer out, and throw everything onto the floor. *I know I had money tucked away in here somewhere!*

"MOM!" I scream as anger and adrenaline take over my body. "Where is it?" I yell as I stomp out into the living room.

"Where's what honey?" She asks all innocent like. I know her well enough to know she's lying.

"The money!" I practically screech. "The guddamn grocery money I've been saving for the past three weeks!" I can feel my cheeks turning red as my temper rises.

"Oh, that money? I had to pay the electric bill; I didn't think you would mind." Liar! I want to scream at her.

"Show me the receipt." I demand sticking my hand out, patiently waiting for her to validate her

41

B.K. Leigh

statement. "Show me!" at this point I'm literally fuming with anger. I'd be surprised if smoke wasn't pouring out of my ears.

"I don't know, Addy. I had Dave pay over the phone." Oh yeah that sounds about right, she had her flavor of the week pay it over the phone... *Bullshit.* She brushes off the conversation and continues to watch whatever soap opera plays on the screen in front of her.

"That was for groceries!" I cry out, before almost ripping my hair out in frustration. I know well enough that the money wasn't spent on our electric bill. Judging by the late notice we received a few days ago we're probably about one week away from getting shut off completely. Now we're going to starve, all because my mother is addicted to smack. I stomp my way back into my bedroom, searching high and low for whatever loose change I can find. I come up with just around six bucks, enough for some milk and cereal. I guess that will last long enough until I can pick up another shift down at the quick stop. *It's going to half to.* I remind myself.

Plopping down onto my tiny twin sized bed I throw my head into my pillow and let out all my frustration. I scream so loud I think the neighbors can hear me, the worn out cotton of my dirty old pillow barley sound proof. After a while my screams turn into tears, and then yawns and eventually I fall asleep completely. My body is exhausted from all of the emotional and physical stress I've put it under in the past week.

Chapter 4

Adeline

I finally wake up hours later to loud yelling coming from down the hallway. My mother must have one of her boyfriends over for the night. *Great.* I check the time on my phone and realize it's already twelve o'clock, thank god for the twenty four hour Walmart we have here in town. I feel like I'm literally starving, after emptying the contents of my stomach this morning.

The best time to go out is at night. Barely anyone is around. Which is great for me considering every time I step out of my house the stares and whispers follow me around. It was fine at school because I had the guys there to shield me, but when I'm alone, it's like putting a chicken in the lion's den. The whole town likes to talk about my mother and what she does in her free time, then they target me as if I'm the spawn of Satan. Sometimes I wonder if I really am.

I search under my bed for my purple chucks and grab some cutoff jeans and a T-shirt from my dresser. I put my ear up to my door and listen. The sounds coming from the other side are almost enough to send me running to the bathroom. It's no surprise to me what my mother has to do to get a bag these days, but I still don't like to hear or be anywhere near it. I walk over to my window and slide the glass up as carefully as possible. With one leg over the sill I pull the other one over and jump down. Thank god we live in a ranch style home, so the drop isn't too far. The harder part is climbing back in.

It takes a while but eventually I make it Walmart. The bright neon sign is like a beacon welcoming me from a distance. I only have six dollars I remind myself as I make my way through the automatic doors, gotta spend it wisely. I take my time roaming up and down the isles basking in the silence... for the most part. The only other people here seem to be the workers and the occasional night owl here and there. I head toward the toiletries with my basket of milk and honey smacks. I know I already have my money's worth but I can't help but look at the mousse and body wash I could have had if my mother didn't take our grocery money.

After minutes of sulking I finally decide to head to the check out. As I come around the corner I slam directly into a massive wall. The basket in my arms falls to the floor with me not too long after it. My elbow connects hard with the floor, and the pain ricochets up my arm.

"Ow fuck!" I screech on impact. I inhale a sharp breath through my teeth, as I try to hold in the tears that threaten to follow.

"Adeline!" his voice comes out sharp and unforgiving as his large man hands come down to grip around my bicep and pulling me to my feet. "Are you alright?" huge black concerned eyes stare deeply into my soul and for a minute I forget he's waiting patiently for an answer.

Snow

"Gideon?" his name comes out like a question and my cheeks heat with fire. "I'm sorry I wasn't paying attention." I turn my eyes to the floor and it's at that time I realize the jug of milk I had has spilled all over the isle floor. "Shit..." I curse as the wetness seeps through the rips of my converse.

"Are you okay? You took a hard hit." He pulls my body towards him and seems to inspect me from head to toe. I bend to pick up the now soaked box of honey smacks when he beats me to it. "Here, let me get it." I watch in confusion as he sweeps the box up and throws it into the mix of items in his carriage.

"Yeah I'm fine, I was just on my way out." I try to bypass him and grab my cereal but he blocks my way like a brick wall. My body ignites with heat in this close proximity, and I have to close my eyes for a second to reign in my raging hormones.

"Let me get that for you." I stare into his dark eyes and try to see where he's playing at. I don't get it.

"No its OK I got it." I try one more time, but watch in confusion as he starts to wheel his way to the checkout only stopping to get a jug of milk along the way with me in tow.

"Seriously, Adeline. I just knocked you on your ass and spilled your milk all over the place, the least I can do is buy you some milk and cereal." My cheeks blush as I watch him throw my two measly items up one the conveyor belt right next to his axe body wash and aftershave.

"Fine." I mumble under my breath, knowing I lost this argument. I shut my mouth and try to swallow my pride. I watch as the cashiers eyes widen with shock. I mean I bet my reaction would be the same if I saw both the town recluse and the towns crack baby checking out together. I turn my attention to the candy section. The little luxuries I was never able to buy, and pick up some peanut M&M's. The cashier tells Gideon the amount owed just as I set the package back down with the others.

"Oh, one more thing!" I hear Gideon say just before handing the cashier a wad of cash. I watch in shock as his arm reaches in front of me just barely touching my chest and grabs for the package of small chocolate candies, adding them to his pile.

"You didn't have to do that" I grumble on our way outside. He bought everything. The six dollars in my pocket are weighing me down like a fifty pound bag of guilt.

"I know." He sounds annoyed. For the first time in minutes I finally lift my eyes to meet his. His eyes look like whiskey. I feel myself dying of thirst just staring into them. I mean whose eyes can turn from chocolate brown, to midnight black, to a cool glass of whiskey? All at once it's like they change colors with his mood, or maybe the time of day.

I don't know what it is, but I can't help my reactions when I'm around him and yet I can get hardly any words out. I watch his lips move and it's as if the noise that comes out is just static to my ears. All I can concentrate on is the glimmer in his irises, the pool of whiskey I'm just dying to take a bath in.

"Adeline?" his eyebrows pinch together. Little lines form around the edges as his eyes squint together.

49

"Huh, what?" I inwardly slap myself in the head over my dumb antics. "What did you say?" we stop walking when we land in front of a huge black pickup truck. My mouth goes dry as I watch Gideon's huge biceps lift the plastic bags from the carriage to the bed of the truck.

"I asked if you needed a ride home." his shirt rides up just a little and I get a perfect view of the dark patch of hair that runs under the waistband of his dark wash jeans. "Adeline?" goosebumps rise along my skin every time he speaks my name.

"Oh um nope, I live just across the street." We both turn our heads in that direction as soon as the lie leaves my mouth.

"You live in a rundown bowling alley?" a smirk crosses his lips as I let out a sigh. Seriously I couldn't have made up something better?

"Yes?" it comes out like a question. Gideon chuckles in return and pulls on the handle of the driver's side door.

"Get in." he stands in front of me one hand on the door the other on his broad hip.

Snow

"What?" I ask in confusion.

"You heard me, I said get in." he points to the empty seat and waits for me to make a move.

"No it's okay really, I live like five minutes away I walk here all the time." I brush off another lie and hope to god he can't see through it.

"Come on Adeline, get in. It's really late and really dark, and I can't in good conscience let you walk home all alone. Now if you can please get in, Max is patiently waiting for me at home." a small smile plants itself across my lips when I remember the huge fluff ball.

"Ugh fine." I roll my eyes and hop up into the cab of the truck. "Let's go, can't keep Max waiting." I mumble.

"So where to?" his smug smile makes me want to smack him, but instead I rattle off directions as we head out of the parking lot. The drive is mostly silent, except for a random direction I spit out every now and again. The air inside of the cab is thick and tension filled.

"It's right at the end of this street." I watch with embarrassment as he pulls his huge truck into the dirt driveway. The big headlight light up my house like a magnifying glass. His face is impassive as I study his reaction. Where Tim lives it's a decent neighborhood. It's where the middle class people of Brookfield with cookie cutter houses and manicured lawns; much like Gideon's himself lives.

"Thanks for the ride." I say quickly as I hop out of the massive truck. I head to the bed and struggle to reach for my small bag that seems to have moved directly to the middle.

"Here let me." Gideon's side brushes mine as his long torso reaches in beside me and grabs the bag I was reaching for.

"Addy?" our heads whip around in unison. My mother stands on the doorstep in just a small robe and a burly man directly behind her.

"Shit." I whisper loud enough for Gideon to hear.

"Addy did you get me cigarettes?" her voice is scratchy and pierces my ears like nails on a chalkboard.

Snow

"You going to be alright?" Gideon's weary voice speaks up.

"Yeah I'll be fine." I make the mistake of looking into his eyes, and all I can see is a tremendous amount of worry. "It's fine Gideon it's just my mother." I force the words out and make a move toward the door.

"And the guy?" his hand creeps out and wraps around my arm stopping me in my tracks.

"Her man for the night." I say with all seriousness. It must shock him because the hold he has on my arm loosens giving me just enough room to break away. I feel his eyes on me the entire way, boring holes through my back like a laser.

"Well?" my mother asks. "Did you get the cigarettes?" her face is earnest.

"No mom, you used the money for a fix, remember?" she gasps in shock as I push my way past her and the random guy to head directly into my bedroom. Feeling overly exhausted as soon as I make it to my bed I pass out like a light.

Chapter 5

Gideon

Figures the moment I step out of my house I happen to run directly into Adeline. She didn't see me as I walked through the double doors behind her, or followed her down each and every isle. I was intrigued by her. The way she moved was as if she was floating, graceful with steady steps.

I watched her as she rummaged through her pockets only picking out spare change. I saw her choosing between the things she needed and the things she wanted. Every time she reached her little hand out for an item, her eyes would fill with longing. I stood there like a statue as her small body turned towards mine, not even moving an inch as she walked directly into me.

She took the fall like a champ. The only problem was the gallon of milk spreading across the aisle floor like a wildfire. It was all I could do to buy her measly groceries. She was standoffish and stubborn but I got my way in the end anyway. The real problem was getting her in my truck. I couldn't with good conscious allow any woman to walk home alone in the middle of the night. I knew where she lived before she told me. I knew enough to know her side of the town wasn't exactly filled with model citizens. I didn't want to leave her at that house, especially when I saw her mother come out side.

Cammy Miller.

Although I made sure she escaped the danger by providing her with a safe way home, I knew her entering that house was the most dangerous of all. I didn't miss the way her mother eyed me up and down. I don't blame her. If I were in her shoes I'd be wary of almost anyone. The burly man standing behind her is no stranger either. Todd Hughes, a shitty guy to compliment a shitty lady. As soon as Adeline walked through the door I couldn't help the overwhelming sense of protectiveness that came over me. Every bone in my body begged to rush in and rip her back out. It was a force to try and get my foot to press against the gas pedal, but in the end logic overcame need.

Having any sort of involvement with Adeline Miller would be a tragedy waiting to happen.

I haven't gotten any sleep. My minds been running crazy ever since Adeline came storming into my life. We were never supposed to meet this way. We were never supposed to meet at all. Things will be worse if it happens again.

Chapter 6

Adeline

It's been weeks since I've heard from Jaimie. All of my persistent texts and phone calls have gone unanswered. Every time I bring it up to Tim and Jake they assure me he's fine, which can only mean one thing… he's completely ignoring me. Not going to lie, that fact does sting a little. Okay it actually stings a lot. I just thought we were closer than that. Apparently I was dead wrong. In the best interest of my friendship with the boys, I decided to forgive them, for the most part. Their constant groveling can't really hurt matters anyway.

B.K. Leigh

Slowly by slowly my mind has been drifting off to Gideon. For the past three weeks my mind has been revolving around his chiseled jaw and deep dark eyes. I can't help but be completely intrigued by him. How can I hear so many awful rumors about one person only to find out they're nothing but lies?

On more than one occasion now Gideon has stormed in like a knight in shining armor. He kept himself at a safe distance, something I wasn't exactly used to. I was scared as hell to wake up in his house, a stranger's house to be exact. I had the instinct to run, but something held me back. I almost had a heart attack when I bumped into him again at the grocery store...literally. My cheeks were red with embarrassment as I slammed into the massive man and then the floor.

"You gonna put something else on?" Jake says as he walks into the living room with a bowl of chips in his hand. His rough voice breaks through my reverie.

"What's wrong with my outfit?" I look myself up and down.

Snow

"Come on, Add's. You've been wearing the same ACDC T-shirt and cut offs for days." Tim speaks up next to me and I punch him in his arm.

"What's wrong with that? I'm just comfortable, I didn't realize I needed to impress our ex fellow classmates." I roll my eyes and scoop up a handful of chips. They both take turns eyeing me up and down.

"Well what am I gonna do? It's not like I brought anything to change into." They both give me a 'yeah right' look.

"Come on, Add's. You've been coming here for years I practically have a drawer filled with your clothes. Besides if you really don't have anything I'm sure you can borrow something of Shelly's." I cringe at the thought of wearing one of Shelly's skimpy outfits. I'm more of a laid back kind of girl, shorts, T-shirts and chucks are more my style.

"Seriously?" I say looking between the two. They nod in unison. "Ugh fine whatever, but I'm not wearing a dress!" I get up from the couch and stomp my way up the stairs, there deep chuckles resonating with each and every step I take.

59

An hour later I'm looking at myself in the floor length mirror on the back of the bathroom door. The black material hugs my body in all the right places, bringing light to curves I never thought I had. My legs are pale in contrast to the dark material. Thanks to Tim's older sister Shelly, I had a whole wardrobe at my leisure. *If Jaimie could see me now he'd have a heart attack.*

"You almost done Add's? It's been fucking forever." A loud knock sounds against the bathroom door followed by Jake's gruff voice.

"Give me a minute Jake, you guys are the ones who said I needed to change." I huff leaning against the counter to put mascara on my lashes. My makeup matches the tiny little dress I'm wearing, black as the night outside. And yes I said dress. Going through Shelly's tiny makeup bag I stop once I find the perfect shade of lipstick. If I'm going to wear a dress I'm gonna go all out. The little tube in my hand say's vixen red, it's just the shade I need to compliment my outfit. I take one last look in the mirror. I barely recognize the girl staring back at me. The only resemblance is the unruly

Snow

curly hair sticking out in almost every direction. I open
the door and make my escape.

"Oh hot damn!" Tim lets out a whistle as I step
foot in front of him and Jake.

"Jesus Christ, Add's. You trying to give me a
hard on here or what?" I blush at Jake's words, and
quickly cover it back up.

"Oh come on guys, you act like you've never
seen a goddamn girl before. Scoot over." I kick at Tim's
leg with my heeled boot and sit down beside him. I feel
the heat of their gaze on me burning my skin. "Uhh Jake
you're drooling, calm down boy." I roll my eyes and go
for the chips again, anything to distract me from there
carnal reactions. If Jaimie was here they'd be dead.

"Sorry Addy, you can't blame a guy for reacting
like this when a female walks in the room dressed like
that." His hand goes up and down gesturing towards my
outfit and my eyebrows pinch together.

"You're such a pig Jake, just finish that and give
it to me will you?" I point to the unrolled joint in his
hand wait for him to finish with anticipation.

61

An hour later a strong buzz runs through my body. The place is packed like a can of sardines. Jake hasn't left my side the whole night, and the alcohol in my blood has me doing things I never thought I'd do. We dance in the group of other teenagers groping and dry humping, my back to Jake's front grinding to the music. I don't miss the subtle looks the boys and girls seem to cast our way. For the last four years this was me and Jaimie bumping, grinding and touching. For this one night I let my imagination play tricks on me. If I close my eyes for just one moment, I'm able to imagine its Jaimie with his arms wrapped tightly around my middle, big hand splayed around my flat stomach. It's messed up and I know it.

"Holy Fuck Add's!" Tim's small frame and bright red hair appear in front of us from out of nowhere. It takes me a moment to focus my haze filled eyes on him. "You guy's wanna come join me?" he points a thumb over his shoulder, and I automatically shake my head yes.

"Come on, Jakey." I pull on his hand and follow the bright red flames in front of me out to our usual spot on the porch. People stare in awe as we pass by, either from my new look, or the fact that Jake was practically just dry humping me in the living room turned dance floor. I smile to myself at the thought of Jaimie's reaction to seeing us three now. It's been a week and we're already almost completely different from how we were when we last saw him. The group dynamic has somehow changed and I'm still trying to decide whether it's for the better or not.

We take our usual seats at the little glass table, with Jake sitting a little too close. The bottle of whiskey gets passed back and forth between us until it's almost empty.

"Do you even know any of those people Timmy?" I half slur. I look towards the windows of the sliding glass doors, and out of the hundred people packed inside the only two I care to know are sitting right beside me.

"Not really." He chuckles. "You doing okay Add's?" he takes the bottle from my tiny fingers. I watch as he slugs the rest of the amber liquid back.

B.K. Leigh

"I'm not really sure, my head feels fuzzy." I tap my head to try to shake the fuzziness away, but that only seems to make the spinning worse.

"Great, we're only an hour in and we already gotta babysit your ass." Tim's words only seem to set my anger off.

"What are you even talking about you don't need to babysit me, I'm fine." I spit.

"Look at yourself, Add's. You're practically falling out of you dress, dry humping Jake from here to China and back and probably a shot or two away from passing out completely." He pulls a joint from his pocket and lights it up. Is it really so wrong for me to want a hit of that too?

"Come on Tim, she's just letting off some steam." Jake chimes in from my side.

"Oh what, like Jaimie will be just letting off steam on your face when he sees all the snapchat's of you two getting a little too cozy on the dance floor?" Tim aim's toward Jake and my cheeks light up with fire. I look to Jake and see a flash of worry cross his eyes.

64

Snow

"Oh lighten up, Timmy. We were just having some fun." I go to stand and wobble on my feet. Being out here with these two seems to be dragging me down. First step is to go find the bathroom, next is to finish my night on a good note.

"Where you going Addy?" Jake asks as I begin to make my journey to the land of the far away bathroom.

"Away from you two pansies, you're dragging my high down." I grumble as a soft chuckle resonates from behind me.

"That's my girl." Tim's voice fades away the further I get, and is replaced with the roaring sound of the bass drum beating from somewhere inside the packed house. Faces blur by me as I stumble my way to the upstairs bathroom, hoping it's not as packed as the one downstairs was. Except for a few stragglers braced against the wall here and there, the top floor is mostly empty. I find my way into the bathroom and close the door behind me. Looking at the girl in the mirror she looks nothing like the brunette bombshell that stepped out of this small room earlier in the night. Her hair is everywhere, forehead lined with a thin sheen of sweat and her bright red lips are smudged. *I'm doing a great job at looking trashy.* I start to dab a piece of wet toilet paper around my lips when the door handle turns.

"Ocupado." I yell towards the wooden door, except the assailant continues to make their way into the small space. "I said it's occupied." I say angrily attempting to push the door closed, but I'm pushed away.

"Adeline Miller." I back away from the looming man in front of me and try to remember where the heck I know him from. My name on his lips sends chills down my spine.

"What are you doing in here, I said it was occupied." I repeat myself for the umpteenth time, all the while slowly backing away from him. His shoulders are broad and he towers above me by almost a foot.

"Just thought I'd come say hi, it's been a while." I hear the click of the lock behind him and my heart lurches in my chest. He must see the look of confusion on my face because it prompts him to continue. "Come on, you remember me right? Scott from chemistry?" I try to rack my brain for a Scott and finally remember him.

"My lab partner?" all this thinking has my brain running in circles. My body's starting to feel sloppy the longer the alcohol is soaked into my bloodstream.

"Ding, ding, ding there you go." He steps towards me and I step back. Something about his demeanor has my heart racing and not in a good way. My hands tug on my dress trying to cover up as much skin as possible, but just the small movement has his eyes flaring with want.

"Well it was nice talking to ya Scotty, but Jake and Tim are waiting for me." I make a move to shove my way past him but he blocks my way and cages me in against the sink. The cool edge of the granite bites my skin as I'm pushed further against it.

"It's not nice to lie Adeline." His breath skirts over my cheeks and it takes everything in me to keep the contents of my stomach down. "I happen to know at this very moment your two body guards are downstairs on the outside deck." He brings a finger up and traces the outline of my cheek.

"They're probably wondering where I am, it's been a while." I push against his arm and he pins me harder against the cold sink.

"Ah, ah, ah." He chastises. "But we haven't had any fun yet." a huge thigh comes between my legs and forces them apart. I try to force them back together but the alcohol has my limbs feeling weak and floppy. I bring my hand up in the air and connect with the side of his face when I feel one of his large hands latch onto my breasts.

"Ah fuck!" his arms leave me for about two seconds and I take that time to stumble towards the door. "You bitch!" I feel the hairs on my head get ripped as my head gets pulled backwards. I stumble hard in my heeled boots, but a strong arm digging into my bicep saves me from landing completely on my ass. As soon as I'm back standing on my two feet I feel the back side of his hand connect with my cheek and I shriek in pain.

"Fuck!" my hand goes up to cradle my throbbing cheek.

"You're not leaving here until I get what I fucking want." He takes that moment to advance on me. His hands are everywhere and anywhere all at once and it's making my head spin. I try to push him off but it's no use, even in a sober state I'd doubt I'd be able to defend myself. I feel the hem of my dress lift up just as black spots begin to crowd my vision. His tongue invades my mouth and I choke on a gag. His touch is unrelenting, making my body shiver in all the wrong ways. I take one last ditch effort to bite down on his tongue and push against his chest with all my might.

"I Said No!" my voice raises to a scream as he stumbles away in shock. The copper taste of his blood in my mouth has me almost doubling over.

"You fucking bitch." His voice is muffles by blood from his cut tongue. It all plays out like a movie. The strike that comes next has got to be one packed with all the force one could muster. I feel my lips break open on impact and I drop to my knees in a clouded state. It takes a while for the room to stop spinning.

"Add's?" I hear my name come through the door and my heart literally leaps in its chest.

"Tim!" I try to yell but Scott cuts me off.

"It's occupied bud." Scott yells towards the door and I hope like hell Tim heard me.

"Is Adeline in there?" Jake's voice is next. I'm still on my knees thanking my lucky stars these two are only feet away from rescuing me.

"Jake!" I try again.

"Addy is that you?" his muffled voice comes in again.

"Listen man I said it was occupied, what's your problem?" Scott opens the door just a crack, and I can see the jean clad legs of my two best friends.

"My problem is I heard a girl who sounds just like my best friend Adeline Miller in that bathroom, my other problem would be the fact that you're in that said bathroom also." Jake's voice went from concerned to angry real fucking fast.

"And I told you its occupied, now take your little fuck boy and get lost." I watch Scott start to close the door when everything before me happens so fast. The door is pushed open from the outside and my two knights in shining armor shove their way through causing Scott to fall off balance. I force myself up from my knees and am immediately thrust into the arms of Tim. I have never in my life been so fucking happy to see someone before in my life.

"Jesus Christ, Add's. What the hell happened?" he says into my hair.3

"I...I was just using the bathroom." I feel my eyes water as the adrenaline in my blood has my emotions sky rocketing. "He wouldn't let me leave, he wouldn't let me leave." I repeat as the first tear falls. Tim brings me into the hallway where a crowd of people have all gathered. Some have their phones out recording the scene in front of them.

"Did you fucking touch her?" Jake yells as his fist connect with Scott's face. "Answer me!" he yells again but Scott fails to answer. Blood from his cut tongue trails down his chin mixed with the river of blooding gushing from his eyebrow.

"Add's? Did this prick fucking touch you?" Jake and Tim both look to me and I bring my hand up to my swollen cheek. It's all I have to do to convey the truth as they continue with their assault. I watch as the two boys beat Scott into a bloody pulp. I watch until I can

71

take no more. I slowly back away from the crowd of people and stumble my way down the stairs and out the front door with tears streaming down my face. The cool night air contrasts against my heated skin. The sting of my swollen cheek feels as if it has a pulse of its own.

With each step I take down the sidewalk, the more and more I'm seconds away from a complete breakdown. My feet can't take me away fast enough and I end of tripping and falling to my knees, no doubt cutting the already sore skin. For a second I allow myself to feel sorry for myself. With my head braced in my hands I let out a stream of tears. I don't know how much time goes by, could be seconds minutes maybe even an hour. I practically jump out of my skin when a huge furry animal sidles up before me thrusting its head in my lap. When I look up I come face to face with Max's big goofy face.

"Max!" I wrap my arms around his head and hug him to my chest. I swear to god I hear him sigh in contentment. "I have had one hell of a night boy." I pull back and rub my fingers through his long fur.

Snow

"Adeline..." I feel his overwhelming presence behind me and sigh in relief. Something about the strange man next-door makes me feel completely safe and at ease. "What's wrong?" I feel him come to stand in front of me and hear the audible gasp on his lips.

"Nothing." I manage to say loud enough for him to hear me.

"What happened to your face?" When I look up Gideon's eyes are storming, black as night and as angry as a category five hurricane. For a brief moment I managed to forget about my throbbing cheek until he brought it up.

"I walked into a door." I lie. I run my fingers over the sore skin and wince in pain. I'm going to have one hell of a bruise in the morning.

"Are you drunk?" his next question baffles me. As if a girl having a mental breakdown on a sidewalk in a ripped dress, swollen cheek, and raccoon eyes is something a sober girl would do.

"What do you think?" I bite out, pushing myself to my feet. The fast movement has me falling forward. I brace myself for the fall but am saved by a pair of strong arms. His body is soft and warm. He smells of fresh body wash and man musk. I close my eyes for a bit and bask in the feeling of him.

"What happened to your cheek?" feather like fingers come down and trace against my swollen skin. I open my eyes and see the worry mixed with fury batting in his deep dark eyes.

"I walked into a wall." I look away as the lie rolls off my lips once again. "It's fine Gideon, I'm fine." He lets me go and puts a foot of space between us.

"Fine, let's get you home." he helps me walk down the driveway to his huge truck and I finally understand what he said.

"Wait! I can't go home." my words come out fast and jumbled. I give him a pleading look. "Please… don't make me go home." That moment red and blue lights appear next door. My heart drops out of my ass. Fuck.

"Well looks like you can't go back over there." he points to Tim's house as kids begin running in all directions as another squad car pulls up.

Snow

"I think I'm gonna puke." My body doubles over almost immediately and lets up all the contents of my stomach all over Gideon's pretty black boots.

"Shh, let it out baby, let it all out." In my drunken haze I almost think he just called me baby. His hands thread through my unruly hair and hold it out and away from the firing zone. My stomach continues to empty its contents when suddenly a rush of embarrassment takes over.

"Please go." I manage to choke out.

"I'm not going anywhere, Adeline. Nice try." His voice is stern and leaves no room for argument but I try anyway.

"Please Gideon just go. This is so gross." I choke on my words while simultaneously trying to push him away. My head begins spinning like a tornado and suddenly I feel myself falling towards the ground once again. The last thing I hear before my eyes close and the blackness takes over is my name rolling off of Gideon's lips filled with worry.

Chapter 7

Adeline

The piercing sun burns through my eyes in the early morning light. My head pounds and my face throbs. I roll onto my side and come in contact with a massive fur ball. Forcing my eyes open the first thing I see is Max's huge body pressed up against me.

"Max?" his name comes out in a question. It takes a minute to remember how I came to be here. "Jesus fuck almighty." I rub my forehead to try to relieve the pressure, but it does nothing to placate the constant throbbing.

Snow

"We have to stop meeting like this." A deep voice pierces the silent room causing me to jump out of my skin.

"Jesus Christ Gideon you scared me to death." I place my hand over my chest and try to reign in my accelerating heartbeat. A small chuckle leaves his lips and is replaced with a smile.

"What happened last night?" I take in Gideon's large form stuffed in what looks to be a small chair by the end of the bed. A tight black shirt stretches across his chest, paired with dark wash jeans that hang just below the V of his waist. The stubble on his sharp jaw makes him seem that much more attractive, if that's even possible.

"What do you mean?" I try to play dumb. I watch as he stands up from his chair and comes to sit right on the edge of the bed right beside me.

"This." his thumb comes up to trace the angry bruise on my cheek. My eyes close at the feel of his touch. "Who did this? Was it the redhead, or his sidekick?" my eyes snap open and are replaced with annoyance.

"No! Tim and Jake would never, they...saved me." the last part comes out in a whisper as the memory of that jerks hands comes to the forefront of my mind. I throw my head in my hands and try to hide the tears that escape like the traitors they are.

"Hey," his large hand comes up to my shoulder. "It's alright, come here." He pulls my small frame into his chest while his strong arms wrap around my shoulders. I lean into his embrace and my hands grip the fabric on his chest. They tears flow freely from my eyes now. There's no holding back. I climb into this strangers lap like I used to do with Jaimie. My arms wrap around him while his rub up and down my back.

"I'm sorry." I pull away and let out a nervous laugh. "I don't know what came over me." I try to move off of his lap but his hands keep me in place.

"It's alright." Our eyes connect. My baby blues against his dark and dreamy ones. One day they're brown, one day there black it's hard to see what color they are in this very second considering his emotions are running crazy like a wildfire. I lean in until we're mere inches apart. His breath skirts over my cheeks the closer we get. We're about a hair's breadth apart, my chest rubbing against his. His hands placed on my hips. My heart races in my chest as my breathing picks up and my eyelids flutter closed.

I feel his lips hover over mine. Just as we're about to finally connect Max chooses that exact moment let out a large yelp. I swear to god he did it on purpose. The damn dog practically has a smirk on his face when he sees Gideon regain control over himself and pull away from me. The hands placed on my hips manage to set me back on the bed beside him and my body instantly floods with coldness. As much as I don't want to, my body feels rejected. As wrong as it seems I wanted Gideon to kiss me. I wanted him to consume me, make me feel something again. I don't care that he's a whole ten years older than me. I don't care that he's been hexed by the whole town. I want him in a primal way. In a way I've never wanted anyone before.

"I'm going to go make some breakfast." He stands on his feet and storms away to the door. "And Adeline, you're staying this time. Come on Max." He pats his leg and the dog besides me jumps off the bed and follows his master out the door and to the kitchen. It takes me a while to regain control of my thoughts and feelings before I'm finally able to get off of the world's comfiest bed. The dress I wore at the party last night is nowhere to be found and in its place is a large black T-shirt that smells exactly like Gideon. I rummage through his dresser drawers until I find another T-shirt and a clean pair of boxers and make my way into the bathroom. I need a shower like yesterday. I feel dirty and grimy and my breath probably smells like dog shit.

I take my time in the shower, using Gideon's body wash and shampoo makes me smell just like him. *Great I've met this man a whole three times and I'm already acting like a goddamn psycho.* When I finally get out I put on his clothes and tie my hair up into a top knot. The T-shirt and boxers hang off me and I rejoice in the feeling of being comfy and warm. My face in the mirror has a little more color to it after the warm water washed some of my stress away. My stomach still aches, my knees are still scraped, and my cheeks still throb. Not even a shower could take care of that mess. Eventually I make my way down the hall and to the

Snow

kitchen. When Gideon's eyes fall on me he has a coughing fit.

"I hope you don't mind," I pull on the hem of the boxer shorts and continue. "I just needed something clean to change into…"

"No, no that's fine." He clears his throat when he's finally able to speak.

"And… I also used your toothbrush." I let out a small smile when is eyes widen in response.

"You're hair looks so… tamed." He decides to ignore my earlier statement; I can't help but laugh at his words.

"Tamed?" We both laugh awkwardly.

"Yeah, uh here, sit down. Let me get you a plate." I sit at the table and wait while he loads a plate up with what looks to be eggs and bacon. We eat in comfortable silence as I wolf down my food in a matter of seconds. The greasy food fills my empty belly and I'm thankful for a morning not filled with milk and cereal.

"You want some more?" Gideon finishes with his plate and grabs for mine.

"Um no thanks." I'm still starving by a long shot, but not wanting Gideon to go out of his way has me keeping my mouth shut. As if knowing my inner turmoil Gideon sets a heaping plate full of food down in front of me again and I smile in thanks. He watches as I load spoonful of eggs into my mouth, practically swallowing the food whole. I didn't realize how hungry I was until real food was placed down in front of me.

"So... once you're finished with that I'll bring you home." I grimace in response as he gets up and goes to the refrigerator. Out comes a jug of orange juice and he pours us both a glass. Breakfast of champions, literally.

"I'm just gonna go back to Tim's." this time it's his turn to grimace.

"You're not going back there." He dead pans. Who the heck does he think he is telling me what to do? What the hell?

"What do you mean? Of course I'm going back over there. I'm staying there for a couple weeks." I pick my plate up and set it in the sink. When I turn around

Snow

I'm chest to chest with Gideon. His closeness has my body on fire.

"What do you mean? Why are you staying over there?" his eyes bore into mine trying to get the answers he knows I won't say out loud.

"I don't know, it's summer and besides his parents are in Europe for the next few weeks, and Tim said I could stay with him." The lies flow out of me.

"What about your mom?" he asks like my mother actually has some sort of say in my life.

"What about her?" I feel his body slowly start to back me into the sink and the painful memory of last night begins to play over in my head. "Matter of fact why do you even care about any of this? It's not like I asked you to come to my rescue, I could have managed by myself." Now I just sound like an ungrateful brat. Obviously I couldn't have made it another day without him.

"I care Adeline, hell if I fucking know. All I know is every time you throw yourself to the wolves and end up black out fucking drunk on my front lawn, I care."

He's so close. He's practically leaning over me. The line of personal space has definitely been crossed.

"That doesn't make any sense." Why would this stranger care when practically everyone else in my life doesn't. His face seems to be getting closer now. The stubble on his cheeks gently brushes against mine as he whispers into my ear.

"It doesn't have to make any sense for it to be true." I chose that moment to follow my instinct. My arms wrap around his neck and I bring my lips up to his. He's hesitant at first, but slowly and surely his mouth begins to move against mine. The kiss is unlike any kiss I've ever had. It resonates all the way deep down into my bones. It vibrates through my chest and all the way to my toes. Once his tongue follows along the seam of my lips I gladly open for him. I swear to god the minute our tongues touch fireworks start to explode in the background. I will admit I'm just a little disappointed when his hands stay pinned on my hips, while mine take the opportunity to explore every inch of his broad chest.

Snow

"Fuck." Gideon pulls away abruptly leaving me momentarily stunned and out of breath. His chest heaves up and down in front of me. His lips are slightly swollen and his eyes are raging with lust. I bring my fingers up to my swollen lips and his eyes light up with flames.

"We can't be doing that." His voice is hoarse but his words hit me directly where it hurts. I'm at a loss for words as I stare back at the only person who's seemed to spark some sort of feeling inside me in a long time. "You're just a kid for godsakes." His hand runs through his hair angrily. His words are aimed towards me but I have a gut feeling there directed more for him. I watch him stalk out of the kitchen leaving me alone, well almost.

"Is he always like this?" I whisper to Max's sleeping body lying on the cool tiled floor. I hop off the counter when Gideon's brooding body comes stomping back into the kitchen. He grabs a set of keys hanging on the wall and makes his way to the door.

"I'll be nineteen in a few months, I am not a kid." I huff, crossing my arms against my chest.

"You needed a place to stay right?" my eyes snap to his in confusion.

"Yeah?" it comes out more like a question than a statement. It's sort of not true. I had a place to stay at Tim's but that was before the cops showed up. No way was I going back there half-drunk off my ass with pigs crawling around.

"Well Max needs to bed fed three times a day, just let him out whenever you see him at the door." the door swings open and he begins to walk away. *What the hell?*

"Wait, where the hell are you going?" I yell after him. Max comes to stand by my side.

"I have business I have to take care of in Boston." He swings a small duffle bag into the bed of the truck leaving me almost stunned in place.

"You can't just leave me here, you don't even know me!" *who in their right mind would let someone they barley know stay in their house completely alone?* He's known me less than a month. This is insane. Jesus fucking Christ I feel like I've been stuck in the twilight zone lately.

Snow

"You needed a place to crash, I needed a dog sitter." He shrugs his shoulders like it makes all the sense in the world. "Oh, and Adeline?"

"Yeah?"

"Try not to throw any parties when I'm gone Max hates strangers." A smirk falls on his lips as he climbs into the driver side of his black pickup.

"What am I supposed to do? I can't stay here, you barely know me!" I seriously can't believe this guy.

"You're the exception. You'll be fine, Snow." And with that he backs down the driveway leaving me staring after him with my jaw practically on the ground.

"Seriously Max, I feel like I just got mind fucked." I call the huge dog inside and numbly walk through the kitchen, down the hall and to the bedroom. *What the hell am I supposed to do now?* Just then my phone vibrates on the night stand beside the bed. When I pick it up Gideon's name is flashing across the screen.

Gideon: You'll be fine, Snow. I'll be back in a few days.

Adeline: When the heck did you put your number in my phone?

Gideon: No house guests, and please just feed Max you don't want to know what he's like when he's hungry.

Adeline: Ugh! Whatever. Stop texting and driving!

Gideon: Calm down it's just Bluetooth, Snow.

Adeline: Stop calling me Snow!

Gideon: Not a chance ;)

Adeline: Fine whatever…

Gideon doesn't respond to my last text so I leave it at that. I eye the giant dog sitting by my feet. His eye brows lift and he lets out a whimper as he jumps all the way up and onto the bed. I don't even know what to do with myself right now. I'm alone in Gideon Wellfleet's house with nothing but his dog for good measure.

I smile thinking about the way he kissed me. The anticipation was agonizing. I thought for sure he wouldn't go through with it. It felt as if his lips fit perfectly against mine. The way they collided against one another was as if they were always meant to be that way.

Not going to lie I snooped through just about every inch of his house, his bedroom, bathroom and living room. His secrets are just about as boring as mine. There are a few unpaid bills here and there and one hell of a hefty liquor cabinet. Max has been following me around with every step I take. I didn't miss the disapprovingly look he gave me as I took a swig from the neck of a bottle of whiskey.

"Oh stop judging!" I mock him as I walk to the living room couch planning to drown out my sorrows with a bottle of jack and some late evening news. It doesn't take long before my eyes slip close and sleep invades my exhausted body.

Chapter 8

Gideon

I've done many stupid things in my life, but at this moment leaving Snow at my house, all alone seems to trump all of them. She's all I can think about as I mindlessly stare into oblivion while my boss rambles on and on. She's one hell of a hot mess and I can't seem to get the feisty beauty out of my head.

"We're going to prolong it until the end of summer." I catch the tail end of the conversation and suddenly my ears perk up. "But that's it as soon as we get the go ahead we're going in and that's final." I've been working with Ryan ever since my first tour over eight years ago. We were a force to be reckoned with out in the field, so when he asked me to work for him it was a no brainer.

"I really don't think she has anything to do with it Ryan, I mean I really just think she's just as oblivious as all of the other victims we've come across." I know I'm fucked as soon as he figures out I have said victim currently staying in my own home. Technically that would be a breach of contract.

"What makes you believe that? You've been on this case for the better half of a year now and have come up empty handed almost every time. What makes you so sure Miss Miller is not involved?" Ryan's been working on this case longer than I have and he's hell bent on getting it wrapped up. As I try to come up with a reason to my logistics I watch Ryan's eyes narrow and then squint. *He knows, of fuck me he knows.*

"Oh for fuck sakes Gideon, you're not screwing the girl are you?" He bites out.

"What? No! It's not like that" I choke out.

"Explain! Now!" he waits for me to collect myself and explain, and reluctantly I do.

"Look, I found her... in my yard." I start.

"You found her?" he cuts in.

"Well technically Max found her... in the yard, I just helped her out. I mean you should have seen her condition I couldn't just leave her out there." for a minute I'm brought back to a different place and time, one where I was faced with a similar decision. It's always the same outcome though. I can never leave anyone behind; it's not in my blood.

"You're telling me you risked this whole sting because you found the girl in your yard? Where is she now?" he asks the question and my throat goes dry. I look away for just a second when I hear him say "Oh for fuck sakes, you still got her don't you?"

"I needed a dog sitter." I shrug. Ryan sits on the other side of the mahogany desk staring at me as if I have just grown two goddamn heads.

"You're kidding right?" he deadpans.

"Not even a little." When I told Adeline to stay I wasn't thinking about the consequences. All I knew was that I wanted her safe. The need to protect her was all consuming, consequences be damned.

Snow

"I guess I'm misunderstanding something here. You're telling me you have one of our suspects currently at your home, with your dog, all alone? Do you want this sting to be compromised? Are you that fucking dumb Gideon? This could blow the whole goddamn operation!" by this time Ryan's up and pacing around the small office in front of me. His face is beat red and I swear sweat droplets are beginning to form around his forehead.

"It's not like that! I have all my stuff locked tight, and besides Adeline isn't like that. I don't think she should even be on the suspect list to begin with." To be honest I knew the minute I got my sights on her she was as oblivious about her surroundings as one could bc. Sure I've seen her with a fair share of marijuana and alcohol, but the shit her momma's been cooking hasn't touched a pretty little hair on her head. I've seen many different types of people over the years, users, abusers, cookers. I know for a fact Adeline ain't any of them.

"You know Bowler is gonna lose his shit over this right?" yeah I knew as soon as Ryan found out Bowler was next, and he wasn't going to be too happy with me. I guess that's a perk of only having to check in every couple weeks though. Maybe by the time I come next everyone will forget about my lapse of better judgment. "Stop thinking that!" he points in my direction.

"Thinking what?" I presume my innocence, but I know he can already read my mind.

"That this entire shit storm will blow over by the time we see you next. Just cause' Bowler ain't in now don't mean word won't get around Gideon. You know I have to report to him, no matter how close we are, my duty to this job and my boss has to come first." I see the indecision in his eyes as the words leave his mouth. I know the job comes first, as it does for almost everyone in this field. We're not supposed to get involved with the suspects in any sort of way; we've all seen firsthand how badly things can end up.

"I know, I know." I take a long sigh. "I'll get rid of her, I promise." I know as soon as I say the words they're just empty promises. There's no way I could send Adeline away. I couldn't watch her self-destruct from far away. At least with her close I can make sure she actually lives to see another day.

Then there's the fact that it almost physically pains me to be away from her. It's like I've been infected by her. Since that first night, I can't seem to get her out from under my skin. They warned me about this, before I took that oath. Demanded I don't get involved with suspects. I never planned on any of this, and now I can't see how the hell I'm getting out.

"I mean it, Gideon. Don't just let some girl from the wrong side of the tracks get your panties in a twist." He lets out a deep breath as he takes a seat once again. "Now that that's over, why don't we go get a drink?" A mischievous grin spreads across his thin lips.

"Sorry, Ryan. You know I'm not into strip joints." His idea of getting a drink is heading to the hefty heifer lounge down the street and banging the first girl that comes into sight. I wonder how his wife would feel if she knew her husband was out getting it on with Jenny from the block. Judging by the wedding band on his hand I doubt she has any idea. While Ryan and I are very much alike in most aspects in our lives, this is where we differ. I'm not into STD's, and he knows it.

"Come on, Gideon. It's just one drink out with the guys. You never get out any more, it'll be good for you." He says while texting away on his phone.

"You know I'm not into that Ry, I'm sorry but I should probably head back for the night." What I really want to say is that I need to get back for Adeline. My heads been going crazy thinking about her. What is she doing? Has she eaten? Is Max driving her nuts yet?

"Earth to Gideon?" Ryan waves a hand in my face.

"What?" I answer.

"So what is it?" he asks.

"What is what?" I must have missed something here.

"Do we have a deal or what?" he waits for an answer as I try to rack my brain for what he was just saying. I must have zoned out completely.

"For?" I ask. I see the moment he figures out I wasn't listening to the thing he was saying. His shoulders drop in annoyance as he pinches the bridge of his nose.

"You weren't listening to a thing I said were you?"

"Not a chance." I reply and he chuckles.

"I was saying maybe I can forget about the whole jailbait thing you have going on, if you accompany me to the bar." He winks.

"You want me to wing man you? What is this black mail?"

"Not exactly." He grabs his jacket from the back of the chair and heads to the door. "Now who's driving you or me?" I roll my eyes. He knows he already has me beat.

"You!" I huff. "But you better have the goddamn jaguar." I say after him.

"Not a chance." He throws my words from earlier back at me. I pull my jacket on and brace myself for a night out with him, dreading the coming hours.

Chapter 9

Adeline

I wake up to the sound of incessant buzzing. Max begins to stir and starts to bark.

"Okay, Okay I'm up." I mumble as the dog continues to make noise. "Jesus Christ Max, stop barking." I complain. I roll over on the couch to find my buzzing phone expecting Gideon but it's not him.

"Hello?" I shoot up in surprise as my heart races out of my chest.

"I've been gone a month and you're already sleeping around?" Jaimie bites out. My heart thunders away at the sound of his voice.

Snow

"What are you…" my voice comes out in fast pants.

"I saw the goddamn pictures, Add's." His harsh words sting. I can't even wrap my head around the fact that he called, my responses are delayed.

"What are you even talking about?" I finally find my voice. The grogginess from my nap earlier disappears completely.

"I saw the goddamn pictures of you and Jake, Add's. I didn't think you'd go whoring around with my best friend as soon as I fucking left." His words feel as if they've come through the phone, strangling me one by one. My heart constricts with anger and most of all hurt. "And with that jackass Scott, seriously two guys in one night?"

"I didn't sleep with anyone!" I yell into the phone. "I don't know what you think you saw but you've got it all wrong." I try to plead with him, but I can hear him seething through the phone.

"Yeah you're right Add's. I do have it all wrong. All this time, you've been playing me and I was just too fucked up to see it."

"What the fuck does that even mean?" I screech. Tears brim at my eyes. I've never once had an argument of this size with Jaimie before, and it's literally taking a heavy toll on my already fragile heart.

"What I'm saying is, I don't want to be friends with a fucking slut anymore." He screams into the phone. His words knock me backwards and it takes all I have not to break down right here and now.

"You don't mean that Jaimie." I whisper.

"Yes I do." He lets out a heavy breath. "I don't think we can be friends anymore, Add's. You've clearly moved on and so have I. I've met someone else, and I think it's best if we don't talk anymore." The line goes dead, and I swear I can feel my heart shrivel in two. I feel a tear trail down my cheek leaving a river in its wake.

Max sidles up to my legs in front of me and rests his head on my lap, his eyes full of remorse. "I don't know what do Max." I say as I run my hands through his thick fur. He whimpers in response, leaning further into me as I wipe my tears away.

Snow

Just then a loud noise sounds from next-door. As I make my way closer to the window it becomes clear it's music. Cars and trucks line Tim's driveways reaching all the way to the end of the cul-de-sac. My mother always said the best cure for a broken heart was alcohol and sex. I know where I can get at least one of those.

*****

Tim's house is literally packed floor to ceiling. As I make my way into the kitchen I'm practically pushed and shoved from all around by kids half-drunk off their asses dancing to the heavy beats. The rhythm flows through me as my chucks bring me closer and closer to paradise.

"Addy!" I hear my name yelled from somewhere but keep my eye on the prize. All I need is a few shots and I'll be good. My hands wrap around a crystal clear bottle of tequila and I swear I feel my body shudder in excitement. As I lift the bottle to my lips, Gideon's face flashes in the background, making me feel guilty for about a second. The liquid gold is cool at first, but burns as it slides down my throat in waves.

101

"Addy!" Jake comes to stand in front of me and a smile forms across my lips. "What happened to you the other night? You just kind of bailed, you alright?" he brings me in for a hug and I nonchalantly inhale his beautiful man scent.

"After what happened upstairs I decided to call it quits for the night and went home." I lie. I bring the bottle up to my lips once more and pass it to Jake. "Here, you look sober." I remark.

"You wanna dance?" he asks, a mischievous smile forming on his luscious lips. Everything seems so much easier when you're drunk. The alcohol flowing through my veins has my body on fire, and my head in a fog. I guess technically I'm a lightweight for getting drunk so quickly, but if anyone knew how much I could consume in a one minute span they'd be shocked.

"Lead the way." My eyes feel glossy as I follow Jake through the tight crowd, until we make it into a corner. "Where's Tim?" I ask. I've been here almost ten minutes and haven't seen my favorite redhead anywhere.

Snow

"Outback with Candy." He wiggles his eyebrows causing me to giggle.

"Seriously? He's been trying to get with her for ages!" he pulls me in until our bodies are glued up against each other.

"Yeah well, everyone needs a little fire in their life." He jokes. The song changes and the beat drops. Couples start grinding; practically dry humping to the dirty lyrics. Our bodies start to sway together, rubbing in all the right places. My legs tingle and my arms wobble as I begin to feel the effects of the alcohol. I feel Jake's arms wrap tightly around my back, holding me up steadily against his rock hard frame. We stay locked together for what seems like forever, until my head begins to swim like a sea of fish. Sweat beads at the top of my forehead. I lift my head off of Jake's shoulder and come face to face with his stormy eyes. I lift my head up just an inch as he moves his down. We're a hair's breadth away I can literally feel him hovering over my waiting lips.

"I want to kiss you." Even with how loud it is I can still hear him whisper into my ear. I feel his hands dip lower and land on my ass, gently kneading the flesh. A moan escapes my lips and his eyes light up like fire.

"So why don't you?" I practically pant. As soon as his lips make their descent towards mine, my boobs begin to buzz. "What the hell?" I say looking down towards my bra breaking contact completely. I take my phone out of my bra and see Gideon's name flash across the screen. "Shit!" I say pulling away from Jake to make my way outside.

"Addy?" Jake yells over my shoulder, but it's too late I'm already out the back door.

"Hello?" I slur into the phone. The cool air feels nice against my hot and sweaty skin.

"Snow?" Gideon questions. "Are you drunk?" he asks, tone demanding as all hell.

"No." I lie giggling to myself.

"Are you laughing?" whoops I must have done that out loud.

"Maybe." I smile.

"Are you drunk Snow?" he demands and I can't help but picture his beautiful face with frown lines etched above his brow.

Snow

"Maybe just a little bit." I burp into the line.

"Where are you?" he asks. His voice has changed and I can't quite figure out what he's feeling.

"Timmy's house." it comes out in a jumbled mess, but makes perfect sense in my mind.

"Next-door? I said no parties!"

"You sound mad Gideon, don't be mad at me. Everyone hates me." I whine into the phone. For a minute I'm reminded of the pain I felt before I came over here, before the alcohol made me forget. "I don't want to be sober, it makes me feel too much." As soon as the words come out I feel myself begin to gag.

"Shit! Adeline? Adeline are you okay?" I hear him speak into the phone as I double over.

"I feel sick." I mutter around a mouthful of vomit.

"Adeline go back to my house, I'll be there shortly." He commands.

"You're lying, you left. You left me all alone. Everyone always does."

"Just get home okay?" he speaks to me calmly now, as if speaking to a small child." I don't have a

105

home, is what I want to say but all I can manage to do is nod my head weakly. I end the call and weakly manage to make my way over to Gideon's house. I swear I stumble and fall a dozen times until finally I make it to the small steps in front of the door.

I sit down for what seems like minutes. The cool cement feels nice against my hot body. My bare legs stick to it like glue. I lean back for just a second, closing my eyes and breathing in the crisp summer air.

"Snow?" I hear someone whisper. I must be dreaming, when I see a pair of perfect chocolate brown eyes stare back at me. "What are you doing outside?" he asks. I smile at his beautiful face. He looks like an angel. I reach my hand out and touch his cheek. It's rough to the tough, filled with a day's worth of stubble.

"You're so pretty." His arms wrap around my body and lift me up in one swift move. He smells of cologne and body odor mixed in one. I breathe in his scent, tucking my nose in his neck.

"Why were you sleeping outside, Snow?" he questions.

Snow

"This is a weird dream." I say out loud. My head is swimming and my stomach churns.

"It's not a dream baby." I feel his lips brush against my forehead and close my eyes. "Are you okay?" He asks.

"I don't feel good." He brings a hand to my forehead and pulls away fast.

"You're burning up, how long have you been outside for? "

"I just needed to sit." I keep my eyes closed as a severe case of spins takes over my body. "Are you really here?" I squeeze out. I open my eyes just enough to see he's walking down the hallway to the bedroom

"Yes, I'm here." He opens the door with his foot, shutting it just the same.

"He called me a slut." My words are still slurred and I watch as his eyes shoot up in confusion.

"Who did?"

"Jaimie." I feel tears fill my eyes and close them once again. "I'm not." I look up to him. "Gideon, I'm not a slut."

B.K. Leigh

"I know baby, I know." He sets me on the bed and I feel my body instantly relax. "Let's get you changed, Snow. I'm gonna grab you new clothes just stay right there." he's back in an instant and I feel his hands begin to undress me.

"Everyone hates me." I whisper as a tear slides out from the corner of my eye. I watch in fascination as Gideon brings his finger to the droplet and wipes it away completely.

"I don't hate you." He says as he lifts my T-shirt up and over my head. I hear his sharp intake of breath as the cool air hits my bare nipples. "Jesus Christ." It's almost inaudible, but he speaks loud enough for me to hear.

"You will eventually." I lay down on my back as soon as I have a clean T-shirt on. "Everyone does."

"Get to sleep, Snow." I feel the blankets come up to my waist, leaving me room to breathe a little.

"Gideon?" I say just before he leaves the room.
"Yeah?"
"Where's Max?" I've come to only feel safe with that big fur ball tucked right into my side.

Snow

"I'll go get him." I watch his shoulders slump as he retreats down the hallway. A few minutes later I feel the dip in the bed beside me as Max settles into his side. For a minute I feel guilty Gideon has to sleep on the couch, but it's gone almost as quickly as it came. My head wonders in all different directions as I try to force myself back to sleep. My body aches and my head pounds. Sooner or later I'm going to have to figure something out. I can't keep living like this. Somethings gotta give.

Chapter 10

Gideon

I feel like it's been years since I've gotten more than two hours of sleep. I've been lying on the couch for the past six hours staring holes into the ceiling. I can't sleep a goddamn wink on this lumpy old couch, and I sure as hell can't sleep for shit with Snow in the next room.

I've gotten up to check on her at least a dozen times already. By the tenth time Max was throwing smug looks my way. I swear he thinks he's her keeper or something. It's not like she has an issue with it, considering she's latched onto him from the first night.

Snow

"Gideon?" I'm broken from my reverie to a small voice standing at the edge of the couch.

"What is it? What's the matter?" I ask, sitting up like there's a fire under my ass.

"I can't sleep." she turns her head away from me. I can see the insecurity rush up her cheeks in a deep blush.

"Isn't Max still in there?"

"Yeah, but he's taking up the whole bed." she sounds annoyed for about a second.

"You want the couch?" I ask. I start to get up but she stops me in my tracks.

"Would you stay with me?" her eyes twinkle as she waits in trepidation for my rejection. Can I do that? I know I should tell her no, but I've been dying to be pressed up against her for days. Ever since I found her, I've had this need growing deep down inside of me.

"I don't think that's a good idea." I say. Her shoulders slump in defeat and a sharp pain forms in my chest at seeing her disappointed. I look her deep in the eyes and whisper the words that will be my undoing. "Only for tonight, Snow."

A small smile lights up her face as her small body comes before mine. I scoot back until my back is pressed up against the inside of the couch. Adeline gets in next, her back to my front and lets out a small sigh. I stay stock still, afraid that once I touch her I won't be able to stop.

"Will you hold me?" it's barely audible but I hear her question as if she's just shouted it through a microphone. Her small hand finds my arm and places it over her side, with my palm resting it against her belly. I guess the decisions made then. A few minutes pass by until her breathing finally evens out. I feel her body relax into mine and I can't help but do the same.

How the hell did I even end up in this situation? Almost a month ago things were still going to schedule. Now I can't even think straight. Adeline's been nothing but a storm, bringing nothing but ruin and destruction wherever she goes. I have to figure something out before I let her get the best of me.

Snow

Chapter 11

Adeline

Sneaking out of Gideon's house proved to be harder to be then I thought. The minute I managed to get his arm off of me I stood up to beeline it to the door. Max wasn't having any of it. I heard his grumbling get louder with every step I took.

"Shhh!" I put my finger to my lips and gave him a serious look. He wasn't having any of it. The closer I got to freedom the louder he got, until he was full out barking. Even when I started to run down the street in the direction to my house I could still hear him barking after me, so much for out of sight out of mind.

The walk home is cold and wet. The rain hasn't let up since the minute I left Gideon's. It takes longer than usual, but by the time I make it to my house the sun is finally starting to rise. I'm relieved and a little exhausted from a long night of drinking. I think I only managed to sleep for about an hour. With Gideon pressed so tightly against me I felt warm and safe. For the first time in a long time I was able to actually get my brain to shut off. I fell asleep almost instantly, only to wake up a short while later. I knew I had to get out of there before everything became too much. I don't want to bring someone like Gideon down. My life is nothing but a hot mess. I can't afford to bring anyone else into it.

A huge pile of black trash bags sit at the end of the driveway, with a swarm of horse flies flying about. All the lights inside my house are on shining bright. The front door is open with just the screen door closed, letting the morning summer air flow in freely. As I walk through the door I'm met with an overwhelmingly pungent odor. The whole place smells entirely of cat piss. I cover my nose with my thumb and forefinger and gradually make my way inside.

"MA!" I yell out in search for her. The smell is nauseating. *When the hell did she get a fucking cat...or five?* "MA!" I try again. As I make my way into the kitchen I begin to hear hushed whispers coming from the basement door. I go to pull on the handle but it doesn't budge. *What the fuck?*

"Ma!" I yell again, banging on the old wooden door. It creaks and bends against my fist, barely holding on against the weight. I hear a slight shuffle and then the pitter patter of feet come barreling up the stairs. The door fly's open in a matter of seconds, crashing against my forehead and knocking me backwards all at once. I land on the cold linoleum floor as my mother's small body stands over me in just a bra and underwear.

"Jesus Christ, Addy. What the hell are you doing home?" her lip curls as she looks down at me. With a shaky hand I bring it to my forehead, only to be met with a pool of blood. The hit from the door must have broken the skin. I bring my shirt up to wipe it away, only to have it begin to trickle down the side of my face all together.

"I left Tim's early!" I exclaim. "What the hell are you doing in the basement? And why the heck is the door locked!" I yell back at her. I have to hold onto the counter as I lift myself off the floor. Dizziness clouds my eyes and has me threatening to fall over once again.

"What are you even talking about? The door wasn't locked, and what do you think I was doing? I was doing laundry." She's lying, I know she is. We don't even own a washer and dryer. Just then heavy footsteps come racing up the stairs and a man appears standing behind my mother. I don't miss the way his beady eyes turn hungry when he takes me in. His eyes are invasive and make me feel extremely uncomfortable.

"When did we get a cat?" I question. Her eyes widen.

"What are you talking about, we don't have a cat." She has to be lying. With the smell emanating through the walls there's no way she hasn't acquired about fifty cats in the last three days.

Snow

"Who the fuck is this broad Cammy?" the man grunts. I narrow my eyes at the man standing against my mother's back before focusing them once again on her.

"That's my daughter Adeline, remember Todd? Jeez, you can be so freaking forgetful sometimes." They banter back and forth while I look on with a confused stare.

"Well, have you told her yet or what?" I cock an eyebrow in his direction. *Told me what?*

"Told me what Ma?" I ask. I fold my arms over my chest in a defensive stance waiting for my mom to answer me. For a brief moment she seems worried.

"Jesus, Todd. You have such a big fucking mouth." She rolls her eyes and opens her mouth. "Todd and I are married!" she waves her hand in front of me showing off the smallest sized diamond I've ever seen. And I'm saying I literally have to squint to see the smallest rock planted in the middle of a faded gold wedding band. My jaw hangs open in shock, but what gets me the most is that I should have expected something like this to happen sooner or later.

"You didn't." I deadpan. My eyes search from his to hers and back again but neither of them cracks a smile. "You're kidding right?" I ask. The cut on my forehead begins to throb with the sudden onslaught of stress.

Her smile falters for a minute. "Jeez, Adeline. I thought you'd be happy for me." she huffs out a breath.

"Happy? I've never even met this guy, do you even know him?"

"Stop being so goddamn melodramatic Addy, it's the twenty first century people have shotgun weddings all the time." This man, Todd puts his arms around her waist and she melts against him like butter. My stomach rolls with nausea at seeing them like this. After all the years my mother had many different men come in and out of this house, the longest has only stayed for the length of the weekend. The only ones I've ever come face to face with are the ones I've accidentally run into while bee lining it to the bathroom in the middle of the night. Not once has one ever shown any interest in making a married woman out of my not so monogamous mother. I can't even stand this anymore. Looking at the two of them is literally making me sick. I make way to go, leaving the two newlyweds staring after me.

"What the fuck is her problem?" Todd nearly grunts in disapproval.

"Don't worry about her baby, she's just in one of her moods." My mother cooed. 'One of my moods' my ass. *What the hell is she even thinking?*

"Are you on drugs or something? What is it this time, coke or heroin?" She has to be off her regular fix to have done something this fucking dramatic. If she thought I was kidding before she's dead wrong.

"Adeline Grace Miller! Todd is you're stepfather now and I will not be having you speak to me or him like that again." she chastises me.

"Drop the stepford wife act Ma, it's not a good look on you." I say while rolling my eyes. When I'm finally in my bedroom I lock the door behind me. It's the only place that offers me any sort of reprieve. I stand in front of the floor length mirror and take in the quarter sized gash on my forehead. *Great. What the hell was I even thinking coming home?* At best I could've just gone back to Tim's, but even then I know I would have the urge to visit the recluse next door. He's not what everyone says he is. That alone makes me want to explore more.

*****

About an hour later I'm fresh out of the shower and climbing through my bedroom window. It gets easier every time. I head downtown to the closest convenience store, seems aunt flow decided to make her grand appearance on practically the worst day. It takes a while, considering my house seems to be out in the middle of nowhere.

"Add's?" I hear my name being called. I turn my head just in time to see my favorite redhead making his way over to me.

"Timmy!" I say jumping into his arms. "How was last night?" I waggle my eyebrows, making him chuckle.

"Jake told you about that? What an asshole!" he shakes his head but a knowing smirk plays at his lips.

"You're such a dog!" I bump his shoulder causing us both to laugh.

Snow

"What are you even doing here? Did you walk?" he follows me down the aisle as he speaks. I hold up a box of tampons and I swear his cheeks flush.

"Aunt Flow's in town."

"TMI Add's, TMI" he blushes.

"Oh whatever Tim, it's not like you've never gotten Shelly pads before, I've gone to the store with you!" I bump his shoulder playfully.

"Yeah but that's different!" he exclaims

"How?" I chastise.

"Because Shelly's my sister, you know my mom would kill me if I don't do whatever she says, and well... you're you." He shrugs his shoulders.

"What the hell does that mean?" We're at the checkout now, and the cashier behind the counters doing a shitty job pretending not to listen to our not so private conversation.

"Well you know..." he mumbles. Red creeps up his neck matching the color of his bright red hair.

"No, Timmy. I don't know." I grab my change from the cashier and put my hands on my hips.

"You're one of us, you know. You're like one of the guys and that's weird." *What in the H E double hockey sticks is he even talking about!*

"Uh, I'm not sure if you're aware of the differences between boys and girls yet Timmy, but I am certainly not a guy!" I screech.

"Okay, okay, seriously Add's calm down." We walk around the corner of the building and her pulls out a small joint lighting it up in one swift move. "I just mean," he inhales deeply. "Obviously Jaimie and Jake get hard ons every time their near you. But like for real though Add's, you're just another one of the guys." He hands me the joint. I take a long pull and hold it in as long as I possibly can.

"Gee, thanks Timmy." I blow the smoke out. "Really means a lot." Handing it back to him I pull my phone from my back pocket. *It's been a few hours since I left Gideon's and he hasn't even tried to call.* I can't help the disappointment that fills my veins.

"Got a hot date or something?" he eyes me suspiciously. Hurrying I shove the phone back into my pocket.

Snow

"What! No!" I feel my cheeks heat with fire. Timmy shoots me a mischievous look.

"Mhm, sure." We walk a fair amount just passing the joint back and forth until it's practically gone.

"What happened with the Five-O the other night?" I ask. I might not remember everything, but I do remember the bright blue and red flashing lights. Obviously it wasn't too bad if he was back at it last night.

"Let's just say I had to do a hell of a lot talking to get out of that one."

"I've never seen those kids run that fast." I laugh and he looks at me funny.

"I thought you dipped?" he asks incredulously. Shit. I can't exactly tell him I spent the night at Gideon's...again.

"I did...it just took a while to catch my bearings." I don't miss the way he looks at me. As if he knows I fucked up and am lying. I don't know why I even try sometimes. He can always tell when I'm lying.

"What the fuck?" I hear Tim say as a huge ball of energy comes barreling towards me.

"What?" all of the sudden I'm knocked backwards. My head hits the pavement hard as my face is being covered in kisses and dog slobber.

"Oh my god Add's, are you okay?" I hear Timmy begin to yell and I force myself to sit up.

"Tim! It's okay, it's just Max." I hold my head with one hand and use the other to run through his thick fur, rubbing him in the spot he loves just above his ear. "Hey Max, hey boy." His tongue comes out to lick my cheek once again.

"You know this dog?" Tim asks incredulously. His hands are planted on his hips and his breathing heavy. If I didn't know any better I'd say he was scared.

"Yeah, this is..."

"Max." I'm cut off by the manliest voice sending shivers down my spine and an ache to my groin.

"Gideon." His name rolls off my lips in a breathless pants.

"Wait, wait, wait. You two know each other?" Tim looks like his heads about to explode in confusion.

124

Snow

"Sort of." I say to my best friend but it only probes further questions.

"What does that mean?" he throws his hands in the air. Meanwhile Gideon watches on in what seems like amusement.

"Do I really have to spell it out for you Timmy? We're..."

"Friends." Gideon finishes causing my cheeks to flush.

"I don't get it." He states lamely. "You guys are...friends?" he points between the two of us.

"That's what he just said." I see the gears twist and turn in the depths of his head only seeming to complicate the situation more and more. Max rolls his eyes.

"Gideon Wellfleet." Gideon holds his hand out for Tim to shake, but he just stares at it dumbfounded.

"Don't be an ass Timmy." I punch him in the arm, practically forcing him to shake the hot man's hand.

"Tim Singer, best friend and bodyguard." He says in all seriousness. Figures he chooses this moment to go all rogue on me.

"Oh my god! Seriously, you're just as bad as Jaimie." I exclaim walking away and stomping my feet.

"Adeline wait! I was only kidding!" *I'm so done with today!* Max comes up beside me following my every step. I don't even tell him to go, just keep speed walking in the direction of my house. As if my day couldn't possible get any worse the rain from this morning seems to reappear out of nowhere. The sky lets loose in a curtain of angry tears.

"Snow!" I hear heavy footsteps behind me as Max lets out a bark. "Snow wait!" long thick fingers wrap around my bicep spinning me around to stare into a pair of the most exquisite brown eyes.

"Let me go Gideon, I just want to go home." I look around him but see no trace of Tim anywhere, so much for that bodyguard.

"How come you left this morning?" his eyes search mine for an answer, and I swiftly look away.

"My mom wanted me home." I lie.

Snow

"Don't lie like that, Snow." His thumb and forefinger latch onto my chin and bring my eyes back to his. My clothes and hair are soaked through, leaving me a sopping wet mess in the middle of the sidewalk.

"I'm not." I try again but it does nothing to placate him.

"What happened to your head?" a soft feather light touch runs across the gash, causing me to close my eyes.

"It was an accident." I say breathlessly. Being so incredibly close to him has my emotions running haywire.

"I don't believe you." He moves towards me just an inch causing our chests to connect in one solid piece. The rain continues to fall from up above in relentless sheets.

"You don't have too." He studies me for another moment. His face moves towards mine inch by agonizing inch. I wait with bated breath, with my heart thundering out of my chest.

"I'm going to kiss you, Snow." He promises.

"Do it." I dare breathlessly. Within seconds his lips descend on mine, turning me into a complete puddle of mush. His arms wrap around my back, as mine hang on to his neck. The feel of him beneath my hands is magical. His muscles are taught and hard. His tongue swipes along the seam of my lips demanding entrance and I happily oblige. I greedily suck on his tongue as his gingerly explores my mouth. I don't want this feeling to end. It's the ultimate high, and I am completely lost to it.

I let go of his neck bringing my hands down to the waist of his shirt. My hands begin to explore the rock hard abs beneath as I try to fuse myself further and further into him. I lift my leg up resting it against his hard hip as a moan escapes my lips with pure need.

"Fuck, Snow!" Gideon pulls away briefly leaving me a needy mess before him. "We can't be doing this." His voice is husky and filled with want. He must sense the rejection flowing through my veins as he quickly recovers. "I mean, we can't be doing this here. People can see." He says as he chuckles against my lips.

Snow

"So let them." I close my eyes and go in for the kill once again but he pulls away all the more.

"Not here Snow, not like this." His body slides away from mine, leaving me feeling incredibly cold. The rain only helps to intensify that feeling. He takes my hand practically dragging me in the opposite direction I was heading.

"Where are we going?" let's face it, at this point I'd follow this man anywhere. I don't think I've ever felt like this before and my body craves more. Gideon is the high I've always wanted to reach. The one I've been searching for.

"My place." He dead pans. I can't help the swarm of butterflies that burst in the pit of my stomach. Gideon marches down the street with me in tow as Max follows close behind.

It's a short walk considering how fast we're going. I barely have enough time to gather my thoughts and feelings before we enter Gideon's house. My back is slammed against the door in one swift move. On instinct my legs wrap around his waist, loving the feel of his manhood pressed up against my most intimate

129

parts. I gasp in surprise. His arms rest against the wooden door on each side of my head caging me in completely.

"Why can't I get you out of my head?" he whispers. He brings his forehead down to mine forcing me to stare into the most soul capturing eyes I have ever seen.

"I'm a disease." I confess. "I bring disorder and corruption everywhere I go. My dad left because of it, Jaimie left because of it, everyone leaves. You'd be best to go while you can." I hear him suck in an audible gasp. His eyes alight with fire, turning them into a dark storm.

"That's not true, Snow." His hands come up to tangle in my hair, pulling at the strands as they rest against my scalp.

"It is." My lips are centimeters away from his, I can practically taste him.

"Let me show you." A shudder runs down my spine as the hairs on my arms stand up in anticipation.

Snow

Chapter 12

Adeline

Gideon's arms move from my hair down to my butt, picking me up and holding my body tightly against his as we move from the kitchen to the bedroom. He gently lays me on the bed, as I stare up at him with hooded lids.

"I'm going to taste you, Snow." He promises. I feel wetness pool in my core, causing my panties to become soaked. "Scoot up." He demands. I crawl backwards towards the headboard as he slowly descends on the bed before me. "Tell me right now that you don't want this and I'll stop." His eyes plead with mine but I can't seem to form the words. Even if I didn't want this, there's no way I'd ever be able to deny him.

"Gideon." I moan as a fingertip traces up the inside of my calf circling around my knee.

"Answer me, Snow." He demands, my eyes shoot up landing on his chiseled chest. My body feels like it's on fire and he's the only one who can satiate me.

"I want you." I whisper as a heated blush rushes up along my neck and my cheeks. He crawls towards me until his body rests completely on top of mine.

"I was hoping you'd say that." He smiles against my lips before taking them against his. I've never felt anything more natural in my life. I've never done any of this but yet with him my body seems to know what to do on instinct. His lips leave mine and travel in an intricate pattern all the way down my body. He takes his time sucking on the sweet spot just beneath my earlobe before ripping my soaked T-shirt off and paying close attention to my bare breasts underneath.

"You're perfect, Snow." His tongue darts out to swirl around my delicate nipple. It hardens and buds underneath his wet kisses, perking up for more. My body practically convulses from all the new feelings and emotions firing through it all at once. I shake and writhe beneath him but he never lets up.

"Mmm, Gideon." My hands fist in his hair as he bites into my nipple, letting go with a hard pop.

"That's it baby, relax for me. Feel for me." His hands slide lower as his body follows. I watch as he unbuttons my cut off shorts, pulling the jean material and cotton underwear down in one swift movement. I'm completely bare to him. Every flaw is completely visible, yet his eyes light up with intense hunger and need. His arms wrap around my thighs as his face hovers just a few inches above my slit. My heart is racing to the beat of its own drum in anticipation.

I close my eyes the moment I feel his hot wet tongue trace along the seam of my slit. His fingers grip into my thighs holding them apart, giving him open access to my core before him.

"I'm yours, Gideon." My eyes roll back in my head as he dives in, attacking the bundle of nerves and sucking my lips into his mouth. "I'm yours." I moan.

133

B.K. Leigh

His tongue circles round and round as I feel my orgasm slowly begin to build in the pit of my core. He's everywhere and anywhere all at once. I feel his tongue travel from my wet hole all the way to my clit and back to my sensitive hole once more. He tongue fucks me as I begin to squirm. One of his arms leaves my thigh to pinch my nipples with his two fingers. The pinch as he sucks and back and forth until I'm a withering mess. I'm almost to the top when I feel an intrusive finger insert inside me.

"Look at me, Snow." He demands. I'm met with a beast of a man. He looks like a hungry animal that's been starved most of his life while he ravages my pussy. "I want to see you while you come on my face." His finger begins to move and all of my reserve crumbles completely. I'm lost to him completely. As soon as his finger hooks upwards my muscles begin to contract and my inner walls begin to spasm. The feeling is blinding and all consuming. Gideon murmurs as my fluids come out in a rush and my limbs shake uncontrollably. My eyes close for just a second until he demands me to open them once again.

Snow

"Don't look away." He commands. My legs are still shaking as I watch him lap up all the juices between my legs. He pays great attention to every ounce, never leaving my lips until I'm completely clean. His fingers finally release me and my thighs slam together. His body climbs up against mine capturing my lips in the most soul binding kiss I've ever had. I can taste myself still on his lips but in this moment I could care less. I've just been eaten out by the most gorgeous and alluring man I have ever met. His tongue invades my mouth connecting with mine in a passionate dance. My hands wrap around his back and hold on for dear life. I can't believe I just gave him that part of me.

He rolls off me, lying on his side with one leg still draped over my naked body. I can't help but give him a shy smile when he looks at me with all the adoration.

"Why do you call me Snow?" I question. He brings his fingertips across my chest to swirl them around my waiting nipples.

"Because your skin is the palest, most pure I have ever seen." He doesn't even miss a beat. The way he looks at me causes me to blush…everywhere. "The only color you have is when you blush, which is a lot." He leans over until his lips enclose around my waiting nipple. My back arches up into him as a soft moan escapes my lips.

"That's not true." I try to lie, but my body tells a different story. He lets go of my nipple and begins to speak again.

"Look." He stares at my flushed skin, mesmerized. "Don't be embarrassed." He hits the nail on the head as my skin turns even darker.

"I'm not." I try to lie but it doesn't seem to work. He shoots me a knowing grin. "Okay maybe a little."

"How come?" he asks, as his lips brush against my shoulder. The way his eyes search mine has me melting into a puddle all over again.

"I've never done that before." I admit. I look away sheepishly before his eyes can catch mine once again.

"Hey," his thumb and forefinger reach up to my chin and turn my head back towards him. "I've been wanting to do that since I first met you." He admits. His lips land gently against mine and I smile in contentment. "There's something about you, Snow. Whenever I'm near you I can barely control myself." His hands fist along his sides as he admits his true feelings.

"I feel the same way. You make me want to do all sorts of things I've never done before." My eyes roam up and down his body, and I'm sure he understands my underlying meaning.

"There's a first for everything." He promises. A shiver ricochets all the way down my spine. I can feel it reach the depths of my soul and break down the garden gates of my heart. Somewhere along the line I've let this man worm his way into my heart, and my body.

Chapter 13

Adeline

"What the hell was that about?" Tim scolds me the moment I walk through his door. Jake sits beside him with a controller in his hand yelling at the giant TV screen before him.

"What are you talking about?" I say as I plop down on the sofa beside him. His eyes bulge as if he can't believe I even have the gal to play dumb.

"You know what Adeline Miller. What the hell are you doing with Gideon Wellfleet?" he scolds me as if I'm a child.

"Seriously Tim, drop the daddy act it's not a good look on you." I roll my eyes.

Snow

"How the hell would you know it's not like you ever had one." He puffs. Honestly there was a time I'd actually be offended but I've had years to get over that abandonment. "I saw you leave with him! I saw him practically drag you into his house." he accuses. My cheeks heat up under the pressure. Images of Gideon tucked between my legs has my heart racing and aching. I'm a complete mess when it comes to him.

"That's not true!" I lie. My eyes wander over to Jake who's watching us as if he's at the movie theater. Only thing that's missing is the bowl of popcorn. "Besides I can do whatever the hell I want Tim, I'm a big girl." I cross my arms like a succulent baby.

"That's not the point, Add's. The point is you can't be whoring yourself out with HIM!" he throws his hands out in front of him. He always was a hand talker. "He's a fucking freak, a murderer!"

"He is not!" I defend. "He is none of those things, they're just fucking rumors." Gideon's been nothing but nice to me. Every rumor I ever heard of him has slowly been put to rest.

"You barely even know the guy, besides how the hell did you even meet?"

"Yeah, Add's. Leave it to you to get with that fucking freak." Jake chimes in from the side.

"Shut up Jake, you're just jealous." I roll my eyes. "You guys don't even know him so you have no room to talk." I cross my arms. No one knows him, at least not like I do. He's shown me a side of him I'm positive he's never shown anyone else.

"Speaking of… Jaimie called here and lost shit on me." Jake stands to walk to the kitchen.

"Yeah well, probably wasn't much worse then what he said to me."

"Seriously! Are you guys fucking too?" Tim stands up in shock, staring down at me like I'm a little kid. His eyes travel between Jake and I.

"No!"

"Not yet!" We both respond at the same time. Tim looks as if he's about to have a heart attack.

"How about never, Jake." How many times can I seriously roll my eyes at someone during one conversation?

Snow

"Yeah right, Add's. You know you're dying to have some of this." Jake grabs his junk and squeezes. It takes all I can to hold back a gag.

"Seriously Jake, put that pencil dick away." Tim scolds him and Jake just laughs.

"What? All I'm saying is if she's giving it to that freak next-door then there's no reason for her not to be giving it up to me." he shrugs his shoulders.

"I'm not giving it up to anyone, now can we please stop talking about what I do and don't do with my own body?" I practically yell at them.

"So you are fucking him!" Tim shouts as he points a finger in my face.

"Oh my god! You guys are freaking relentless."

"We're only kidding Addy, just don't want to see you get hurt." I know Tim's dead serious. Ever since we first became friends all he's ever done is look out for me.

"You're just going to have to trust me when I say nothing's going on." I lie. "He's not what you think he is." I look past Tim, and see Jake's eyes darken

141

B.K. Leigh

slightly. An uneasy feeling sinks into the pit of my stomach.

"I don't believe that for one minute." Jake snickers.

"Seriously Jake, take the stick out of your ass." I rise to my feet and stretch my hands above my head. I turn toward the stairs.

"Where are you going?" Tim asks.

"I'm going to bed, I'm exhausted." I yell over my shoulder.

"Yeah too much sex can really tire someone out." Jake snickers.

"I heard that!" I yell just before reaching the top of the stairs.

I've slept in Shelly's room a million times, but for some reason it just feels different. My body aches to be next to the man next door. Knowing he's only a few feet away has my body throbbing to be closer. I was nervous when he left me alone. And scared when I realized how badly I fucked up. I didn't think he'd look twice at me, after I practically threw up all my insides all over him, his shoes and his house. And that was just the first instance. I can't even imagine what he thought of me when he found me half dead on his front steps. I thought he'd want nothing to do with me. I thought he'd make me leave so I did the next best thing and left before he could say anything.

I wasn't planning on seeing him again, at least not for a while. When he caught me on the sidewalk I was confused, and torn. The best thing for both of us would have been to walk away, but something about Gideon has me coming back for more and more. It's not a coincidence I just so happened to end up at his house. Even in my drunken haze I knew what I was doing.

I'm staring at the ceiling as my phone buzzes from beneath my pillow. I take it out, blinded by the light and try to read the name that's flashing across the screen.

Gideon: Can't sleep?

I look all around me. The curtains are closed and the doors locked, there's absolutely no way he could see me.

Adeline: How the heck did you know?
Gideon: I have my ways ;)

Here's the part where I don't know how to reply. I never had to flirt with Jaimie; we just sort of had an unspoken mutual agreement. My heart races as the three dots light up my screen.

Gideon: I've been staring at the ceiling for hours, thinking about you.

I smile to myself in the dark.

Adeline: What are you thinking about?

I turn on my side and look at the words on the screen. Is Gideon lying in his bed like I am? Is he dying of anticipation? Is this just some stupid school girl crush, or could this be something more. I keep replaying the images of him bringing me to my first orgasm. The way he took control and manipulated my body as if I was a puppet and he was the puppeteer was all consuming.

Gideon: The way you taste, the way you moan. The way your thighs tighten when I press my tongue against your clit.

I can feel myself getting wet just thinking about it. My body starts to tingle thinking of all the way's Gideon made me feel good.

Adeline: You sure don't hold anything back.

Snow

I try to make it seem lighthearted. Flirting doesn't come easy for me, it's not exactly in my vocabulary. I don't understand how Gideon can be so brazen.

Gideon: Neither do you ;)

His words make me flush. I'm alone in someone else's bedroom in the complete dark, blushing from head to toe.

Adeline: I don't know what to do with any of this.

I shamelessly admit. My heart pounds as I wait for his reply.

Gideon: We'll figure it out, Snow. But for now go to bed.

His reply makes me feel a little dejected, but I let it go anyway.

Adeline: Night, Gideon

Gideon: Goodnight, Snow.

If I couldn't sleep before, my insomnia is even worse now. Gideon's a drug. He's invaded my body and my mind, taking over my very being. His words fill me up, putting my body at ease and my mind to rest. All the high's I was chasing before don't even compare.

Chapter 14

Adeline

"What are you staring at?" I try to look away as quickly as possible, but Gideon catches me anyway. I can't help it. My eyes drift over to him on their own accord. His black hair is sticking out in every direction. I've watched him run his hands through the silky strands at least a dozen times. My throat runs dry almost every time.

"Nothing." I turn my eyes towards the window and try to focus on something other than the beautiful giant sitting beside me.

"You're such a bad liar, Snow." He flexes his fingers around the steering wheel. It feels as if he's squeezing my heart. I swear I can feel each and every digit digging into my flesh. A few minutes pass by before he speaks again. "You're staring again, Snow."

"I can't help it." I sigh exasperated. "You're sitting over there all smug like a freaking Greek god." I lift my feet up and rest them against the glove box. Every few feet the purple fabric of my chucks light up against the brightness of the street lamps outside.

"Feet down, Snow." Gideon reprimands me as if I'm a little kid.

"Fine!" I practically whine crossing my arms over my chest like the baby I am.

"Seriously Snow, what the hell is bothering you?" I didn't realize anything was bothering me until I was forced to sit in the passenger side of his brand-new truck for the past hour. Well, I mean I wasn't exactly forced. More like I forced Gideon to let me come with. But what I wasn't anticipating was the radio silence.

"Nothing!" I lie. My voice raises a few octaves, giving me away. I feel the truck start to slow down and begin to worry as we pull to the side of the road. We're in the middle of nowhere with nothing but corn fields

on either side of us. Its pitch black outside. I watch
Gideon's bicep flex as he practically slams the truck in
park and turns towards me, eyes storming.

"We're not going anywhere until you tell me
what the hell is up." His voice is coarse. The smell of him
permeates through the entire cab, cologne mixed with
his body soap. I breathe in deeply and sigh in relief.
Something about it puts me at ease.

"I don't know, I mean, I just thought that maybe
you'd talk to me." Gideon seems to only be able to talk
to me through text lately and it's utterly annoying.

"I'm talking now aren't I?"

"Yeah but that doesn't count. You're only
talking cause' you think I'm mad at you or something." I
shrug my shoulders.

"Are you?" he asks. "Is my Snow mad at me?"
he pouts making me laugh.

"No I'm just..."

"Frustrated?" my eyes snap up to his. He hit the
nail on the head with that one. "Are you frustrated
because I won't talk to you? Or because I haven't
touched you since I ate your pussy?" his dirty words

149

make my cheeks flush. My core begins to ache and my breathing picks up speed.

I nod.

"Are you aching to be touched by me? Do you want my lips on yours so fucking bad it hurts? Are you thinking about it right now, how it would feel to have my lips on you once again?" his lips are just inches away from my ear. Every other word I can feel them brush against the sensitive skin there. He's so close I can practically feel his chest against my side.

"Yes." I close my eyes and whisper into the darkness.

"Tell me." he demands. "Tell me you want it just as badly as I do." He takes a deep breath. "That the thought of being with me has been tearing you up inside, consuming your mind body and fucking soul as badly as it has been mine." His hands come out and grip my hips. In one swift movement he lifts me up and places me right on his lap, each of my thighs rest against the outside of his. Through the fabric of my jean shorts I can feel his thickness swelling against my core. It's throbbing and heating with need.

Snow

"I do." I moan as he starts to rub against me. "I want you so bad it hurts." How do I tell him I've wanted him since the first time I laid eyes on him? That the mere thought of his body against mine has been plaguing my thoughts since that first night out on the deck. I was enamored by the thought of him, intrigued by him alone, and turned on by the dangerous aura that seemed to follow him wherever he went.

"Fuck, Snow." His hands come up to tangle in my hair and he forcefully pulls me into him. My lips smash against his in a hungry kiss. His mouth consumes me completely. I can feel every last heated emotion flowing between us, anger, frustration, want and need. His hips grind into my in a rhythmic manner. The fire within is burning fiercely and out of control.

It's uncontainable.

It's uncontrollable.

"That feels so good." I mewl between kisses. The fabric of our jeans rubs against my core in just the right way, causing a burning friction to build up.

"Tell me how badly you want it," he demands between kisses. "Tell me how bad you want this…us."

our tongues dance together it's hard to get any words out. I don't want to stop for one minute but for Gideon I do.

"I want it Gideon, so damn bad." He takes hold of my hips and begins to rock me back and forth. His hands guide me to exactly where I want to be. Our breathing picks up together. The windows are completely fogged up shielding us from the outside world.

"Come on baby, just a little more." His voice comes out strangled. His eyes cloud with lust. The feeling deep down inside of m begins to overflow. My clit is being rubbed in just the right way, just one more time and…

"Gideon!" I practically yell his name as my body spontaneously combusts from the inside out. He lets out a strangled cry of pleasure and I can feel the sudden hot wet spurts push against his jeans.

"Fuck, Snow. You're killing me." he rests his head against my shoulder. Our breathing mixes together, our foreheads are hot and sweaty. My body is completely spent as I try to slide off of his lap. My legs are sore from being spread apart for so long but it was completely worth it. He leans over to place a chaste kiss against my lips and I can't help but smile against him. I feel myself willingly hand over another piece of my heart to him. At this point I can only pray he handles them with care.

Chapter 15

Adeline

"Need something?" a deep voice says from behind me. I turn around only to find my mother's new husband standing a little too close. His back is against the counter and his belly is sticking out. His jeans scream in protest as his fat pouch pushes against them. My stomach roils at the stench wafting off of him. My hand rests on the basement door handle as I turn to speak to him.

"I was just looking for my mom." I lie. I thought if I could sneak down stairs I could figure out what the hell they were hiding. The doors been locked for weeks, but today they forgot... or at least I thought.

Snow

"She's not home." he states.

"Where is she?" I can't for the life of me remember a time when my mother actually left the house...alone. She's had me go to the store for her for as long as I can remember. I narrow my eyes.

"Where did she go?" I ask. My voice sounds accusing and I watch his body language shift from creepy to high alert in a matter of seconds.

"Out." Just one word.

"Fine, I'll just call her." I reach for my phone as he takes a fast step forward.

"I said she was out. There's no need to be calling her." His words are laced with anger. I take a step away from him, eyeing him suspiciously. *What the hell is wrong with this guy?*

"Okay..." I draw out the word. I go to walk around him but his hand whips out and grabs my arm.

"I don't want to see you near that door again." his face is red. "Your mom won't always be here to save you from the consequences." Yanking my arm from his grasp I hurriedly walk away. I hear his warning loud and clear. Whatever the hell is in that basement is top secret.

Chapter 16

Adeline

"I have to leave in the morning." Gideon says as he tugs a shirt over his head. I try not to hide the disappointment I feel. We've spent the better part of the morning making out among other things. "I want you to come with Me." he searches my eyes for an answer. I can't reply fast enough.

"Yes." I reply shaking my head. "Yes, I'll go!" I kiss his lips once again but he pulls away too fast.

"But you don't even know where we're going yet." He chuckles.

"I don't care." I exclaim. My body feels light as a feather as his fingertips begin to trace the apex of my thighs once again. I don't budge, at this point I'd let him do whatever he wants to do to me.

"Fine, since you don't seem interested in knowing at all, I guess I'll just tell you." His eyes sparkle like a little kid waiting for an ice-cream cone. "I have a house in the cape; I need to take care of a few things there for about a week or two. You sure you're up for it?" what I want to do is jump in his arms in hopes he'd take me away forever, but I know that's asking too much. I try to reign in my excitement as best I can but fail miserably.

"The cape, as in Cape Cod?" I practically squeal. I've never even been to the beach.

"The cape as in Cape Cod." He confirms with a smile on his face.

"And you want me to go with you?"

"Almost too much." He replies in a whisper. I bring my forehead to his until they're resting against each other skin to skin.

"When should I pack?" a huge smile spread across his face matching my own.

Snow

"We leave in the morning. You sure you want to come?" for a quick second worry clouds his beautiful face.

"I've never been surer of anything in my life." My words mean more to him than he will ever know. In this short period of time I feel like I could possibly have met my other half. I knew what I had with Jaimie had been strictly platonic. Even though we liked to push the boundaries, we always knew how it would end up.

"What about your mom?" he asks.

"She'll probably be happy to have me out of her and her new husband's hair for a bit." his eyes scrunch up in confusion.

"New husband?"

"Yeah, I found out a couple weeks ago. The guys a real creeper." I roll away from him and off the bed completely. I spent the night again last night. Something I've begun to make a real habit of. No matter how badly I try to break it, I always come back. Tim and Jake have tried to warn me, but it's no use, I'm a goner.

"Where are you going?" he calls after me.

"I'm taking a shower," I wiggle my eyebrows. "Why you want to join me?" I'm only half hoping he says yes, and am completely relieved when he declines my offer. Sex is a big thing. Sex with Gideon would be an even bigger thing. I'm not sure my heart could handle something like that so quickly.

"There's a T-shirt and shorts on the bed for you when you get out." he knocks a couple times on the bathroom door. I smile at his gesture. He's always taking care of me.

"Okay, thank you." Regretfully I resume back to my shower, washing Gideon's scent away from my body and down the drain. The water is warm and kneads my muscles in soft beads. I take my time, enjoying the hot water as best I can. My nerves are getting the best of me the more I think about spending a whole week with Gideon all alone. I've spent the night with him almost every night for the past month but the unknown is what's eating at me. Summer is practically coming to an end; will he still want me when it's over?

I start to wonder how a man like him could ever be attracted to me. Not only am I lacking in good looks and charm, but I'm from the complete opposite side of town from him. He's old money, and I'm no money. How is that even remotely appealing to him?

With Tim, Jake, and Jaimie we all had common ground. Sure we all lived on different sides, but there was a middle ground. Technically weed brought us together as fucked up as that sounds but we stuck together like glue after that. Through all the rumors and setbacks we never faltered.

Is that how it will be with Gideon, will he still want me when he sees where I come from? Yeah he's seen my small shack of a house, but will he still want me when he finally meets the girl who lives inside? When I told him I was a disease I meant it.

Chapter 17

Gideon

I knew right away I'd never be able to last a couple weeks without her. I have no other choice but to ask her to come. To be honest if she had said no, I wouldn't be opposed to begging.

When my parents passed away, they left me practically everything with the sole contingency being I take care of Max along the way. So every summer I make sure to spend a couple weeks up at their old beach house, keeping things up to date and running. It's a small two bedroom cottage right on the bay. I have no doubt Snow is going to love it. The downside will be trying to keep Ryan off my back for as long as possible.

Snow

He told me Bowler wouldn't move in until the end of summer, and I took his word for it. Bad thing is we only have a few weeks left.

"You ready?" I ask Snow, who seems to be staring at the house before us. She seems nervous but she insisted on picking up a few things before we left.

"Yeah, I just gotta pack a bag real quick." She hops out of the truck before I can even reply. I catch up to her just before she walks through the screen door.

"Your mom home?" I ask as I take in my surroundings. The odor is strong and I know right away this is definitely the location of their lab. The garbage pile outside was the first indicator. The smell and the bare walls inside was the second.

"She's somewhere." She shrugs a shoulder seemingly unfazed by everything around us. It's eerily quiet, something I was entirely not expecting. I follow her slim figure to a wooden door at the end of the hallway. As soon as I step foot into her bedroom, my eyes dart from wall to wall and stop directly on her. There's a padlock on the door. I'm fixated on it as she turns the key and locks it in place.

"Precaution." She quips. As if it's the most normal thing in the entire world to have a lock like that on the inside of someone's bedroom. Her space is small yet accommodating. She has the bare necessities. It seems lifeless, much like Snow herself. The smell doesn't seem to wrap around the room like a contagious disease, unlike the rest of the house. It's a good sign, considering Adeline seems to be at the top of Ryan's suspect radar. The less footprints leading to her the better.

"For what the apocalypse?" I kid, but her face is stock still.

"My mom has a lot of boyfriends." She goes over to a small dresser and starts rummaging through the drawers one by one.

"I thought you said she was married." I mentally take note adding it to the list of things I'm going to tell Ryan later on tonight.

"Yeah, recently as a few weeks ago" She stuffs the small pile of clothes she collected into a ratty old purple bag, my eyebrows quirk up in disgust. "It's my favorite!" she defends herself holding the bag tightly to her side as if I might take it away from her.

"I didn't say anything!" I chuckle as her cheeks heat up with fire. We head out of her room back towards the front of the house where we came in.

"Hey there pretty lady." Snow's shoulders tense before she stops in the doorway of the kitchen. I purposely stay a few steps behind, waiting in surprise.

"Is my mom home?" Snow asks sharply.

"She's down stairs doing laundry." From the shadows I can see the way his eyes leer at her. "Did you need anything?" the fat bastard literally licks his lips as his eyes travel up and down her body.

"No she's all set." I came up to stand behind her. Just like I suspected his eyes widen in first surprise and annoyance. I rest my chin on her shoulder while having a mental showdown with the man before us. Her body relaxes into mine as a small smirk forms across her lips.

"Who are you?" he puffs out his chest, spreading his feet apart and crossing his arms across his potbellied chest.

"I'm," before I'm finished, Snow cuts me off completely.

"My boyfriend." She states loud and proud. I have to mask my shocked expression. It's all a game, I remind myself. She doesn't mean it. The man's eyes glance between us in a questioning manner. "Tell my mom I'll be home in a few days." She seems to have found her confidence as she grabs my hand and drags me towards the door. We hop in the truck not a minute later, with her mom's husband watching from the doorway. Snow was right, he is a creepy bastard. But what she doesn't know is that this guy has one hell of a rap sheet.

"My new step daddy." She nods towards the door while rolling her eyes.

"You don't seem too thrilled."

"Would you be?" she asks.

"Absolutely not." I shake my head at her.

"How long have you lived there?" I ask nonchalantly. I need more information. I need to know for a fact she has no idea what kind of operations is going on directly under her nose. You'd seriously have to be as blind as a bat to not have any indication. Or in her case you'd have to be completely high or drunk at least ninety percent of the time.

"All my life." She pulls her knees up to her chest as she watches the trees pass by out the window.

"Just you and your mom?"

"And her endless supply of one night stands." She tucks a stray hair behind her ear. "Until now, that guy gives me the creeps." She shivers for emphasis causing me to chuckle.

"Yeah, you're not kidding."

"What about you?" she inquires.

"What do you mean?"

"Have you lived in your house since you were a boy?" her eyes burn a hole through my head as she waits for me to answer. Since when did this get turned around on me?

"Since I was a baby," I smile at her before turning my attention back to the road. "Max, too." As if on cue the big goof whimpers from the back seat. Memories of endless summers and holidays with my parents come flooding back all at once. I've tried so hard to leave it all behind me but sometimes it sneaks up when I least expect it.

"What were they like?"

"My parents?" she nods her head yes. "My mom was the most amazing woman I knew. She was intelligent, kind and loving. She home schooled me most of my life. It's one of the reasons I decided to go into the service. I never knew what true friendship and brotherhood was until I saw it first hand out on the field." She listens intently as I continue. "My dad was the cook in the family. My mom couldn't cook for shit." she laughs at that and I feel my heart fill with joy. "He was a great man. I used to walk around in his huge boots, thinking if I wore what he did I could be just like him. I only ever wanted him to be proud of me." I sound like a sap. But every time I speak about my parents, I can't help but let all of the feelings flow.

"I have no doubt they would be." She says with conviction. My heart constricts an inch.

"You think so?"

She shakes her head before replying "Definitely."

Snow

"The beach house was my mom's favorite place in the whole world. You're going to love it there." I squeeze her thigh gently and she gives me a shy smile in return.

We spend the rest of the drive with me reliving most of my past and her listening contently. A small part of me feels guilty for lying to her. But the bigger part argues it's what's best. I can only hope that when it comes down to it she doesn't hate me.

About half way through I manage to turn the conversation around back on her. She tells me some of her darkest secrets. Things about her mom, her friends and her life all spill from her lips. She tells me them in confidence as I mentally take note, knowing I'm going to have to expose each and every one of them once I speak to Ryan. I might keep the one about me being the first to eat her out to myself, considering my jobs on the line.

After a fair amount of talking she leans her head against the window and I watch as she slowly begins to fall asleep. Her breathing evens out and her eyelids flutter closed. She seems so at peace, that I barely have the heart to wake her once we arrive. I send a quick text to Ryan letting him know we have to talk. I take one last look at Snow's sleeping body and pray she'll forgive me for what I'll eventually have to do. My only hope is that it happens later rather than sooner. The worst part of all is that I think I'm falling for her.

Chapter 18

Adeline

I wake up to Gideon's soft voice at the shell of my ear, sending ripples of shivers down my spine. "Wake up, Snow. We're here." He pulls away just as my neck and cheeks turn red. I raise myself up from my sitting position and take in my surroundings. I'm in complete awe as I take in the scenery around me. We have to be at least one hundred feet away from the soft ocean waves lapping at the sand before it.

"Holy shit!" I say hoping out of the truck and heading straight towards the water. The beach goes on for miles and miles without another soul in sight. My feet stop at the edge of the sand as I squat down and run it through my fingers. I feel like a little kid in a candy shop. Never in my life have I seen a sight more beautiful than this. I'm completely captivated.

"You like it?" Gideon asks from behind me. I take no time untying my purple chucks and throwing my socks to the side.

"You didn't tell me you live on the freaking water!" my smile must be contagious, because the one on Gideon's face is stretching ear to ear. I wiggle my toes through the sand and squeal in excitement. I head towards the water like a fly drawn to a lamp.

"Where are you going?" I hear him call out to me, but I'm completely lost to the sight.

"To the water." I pick up my pace with Max at my heels. This is literally the best day ever.

"What about your bathing suit?" he yells.

For a minute I stop in my tracks. I turn around to reply only to find him directly behind me, entirely shirtless. My throat goes dry, and my core starts to ache with need.

"I don't have one." I squeeze around the lump in my throat.

Snow

"We'll go shopping later for food and grab one while we're out." he promises. I nod my head in return, turning my back on him once again. His hand whips out gripping my arm like a snake striking its prey, fast and precise.

"Snow." My nickname rolls off his tongue in one fluid motion. I swear if he wasn't holding me up, I'd be putty at his feet. His chest leans into mine as I tip my chin up to meet his penetrating eyes. "I'm going to kiss you now." He dead pans.

"Do it." I push up onto my tippy toes and meet him halfway. I can't even explain the rush of emotions that explode throughout my body as soon as we touch. A spark of electricity flows through my veins as his lips mesh with mine. His tongue darts out as I grant him open access. His lips are soft. Every kiss is as if he's making love to my lips with his mouth. His hands slide down to the edge of my T-shirt and slowly begin to lift it upwards.

"What if people see?" I dart my head around, but see no one else in sight.

173

B.K. Leigh

"I own the beach, no one else is around, and if they are they're trespassing." He shrugs his shoulders while nipping at my lips.

"The whole beach!" my voice raises a few octaves. Seriously can this get any more freaking better?

"The whole beach." He nods his head as he dips it into the crock of my neck, nipping at the supple skin below my ear. "You going to stand here ogling all day or are you going to get your ass in the water?"

"Let's go." I pull on his hand but he lets go, latching onto my hips and throwing me over his shoulder. "Hey! Put me down, Gideon. I can walk myself!" I hit his back and wiggle my hips but he just holds on tighter.

"I don't know about that, Snow. I feel like I just grew gray hairs waiting for you back there."

"You're the one who kissed me! If it was such an inconvenience maybe you shouldn't do it anymore." I whine against his chiseled back.

"We both know there's not a chance of that happening Snow." His feet break against the water as

Snow

my body fills with adrenaline. I can feel the water droplets as they bounce off the backs of his feet the deeper he wades.

"You can put me down now!" I complain.

"Oh I'm going to, Snow. Hold your horses." He takes a quick pause. "You can swim right?" he asks in all seriousness.

"Yes?" although I've never been to the ocean it doesn't mean I've never swam before. Thanks to Tim's mom and dad, I've had full access to his ginormous pool for the last four years.

"Good!" in one swift motion I'm sent flying through the air. My body breaks against the freezing ocean water as Gideon laughs in the background. My butt hits the ocean floor as I'm completely emerged, a smile literally still plastered on my face. There's nothing like the feeling of ocean water. I could care less if I'm most likely getting frostbite in all the wrong places. I come roaring back up to the surface when my lungs thirst for air.

"That was not funny!" Gideon holds his belly laughing at my appearance. I look like a wet sewer rat.

My usually frizzy curly hair is now flattened and plastered against my skin.

"You loved it!" he gives me a 'know it all' look. And he's right, I did. I don't even have to ask before he does it again and again. We spend the better half of the rest of the day swimming around and walking along the water line. I'm a little kid at heart and stop to pick up all the seashells and pretty rocks along the way. Gideon tells me stories about him as a boy, only seeming to add to my vision of him as a little boy from the ones on the drive here.

It's not until a few hours later until we finally make it inside, sun fried and sandy. The house is as spectacular inside as it is outside. Everything resembles the beach. The walls are a soft blue with matching sandy colored counter tops. Small accents hang on the walls only seeming to tie everything together. The bedrooms were the last stop on the grand tour. Two large rooms sat side by side, and if we were smart there'd be one for each of us. But I never claimed to be smart.

Snow

"This is my room." Gideon says as he takes in my expression. "And yours." He eyes me intently waiting for my approval. A swarm of butterflies take off in my chest.

"Okay." I whisper.

"Why don't you take a shower and get dressed while I cook us up some lunch?" He kisses my bare shoulder, sending goose bumps down my arms. I can only nod in response. This day has been one out of a fairytale and it's only half way over. How I managed to even end up here, I'll never know.

Chapter 19

Adeline

We've been at the beach house for almost four days now, and there's been nothing but radio silence from Gideon since that first day we arrived. We sleep in the same bed at night but couldn't be further away in reality. I spend my days lounging on the beach in the tiny bikini Gideon bought me the first night we were here. Sometimes I'll bring Max for walks, or just sit out on the sand and read one of the many books I grabbed from the massive bookshelf inside. Gideon's like a ghost. Here one moment and gone the next. Every once in a while I'll see him working on some sort of odd jobs around the house but other than that he seems to be completely stuck inside himself. I can't really complain considering he was nice enough to invite me along, but I guess a part of me feels let down by the lack of attention. After a long day outside in the sun I decide to head inside.

"Gideon?" I call out. With all the sunlight streaming through the open shades the house feels incredibly dark. "Gideon?" I try again, walking slowly from room to room. I stop by the door of our shared bedroom, my heart longing to do more than just sleep bedside him.

"What are you thinking?" a masculine voice whispers into my ear from behind. I feel his strong body nestle up against mine and I relax into him completely.

"Where were you?" I side swipe his question, as his hands begin to trace up and down my stomach.

"Tell me." he demands, ignoring my attempt at changing the subject.

"Why haven't you talked to me?" I ask in a small voice.

"That's not what you wanted to say is it, Snow?" he trails his fingertips up and down my arms. I lean my head back against his chest and bask in the feel of my body against his. "Is it?" he knows he's right. He's the only one who seems to be able to read me like a book.

"Why haven't you kissed me?" I seem to get my courage back the more his finger explores my body. I shudder in anticipation as one finger dips below the top of my bottoms.

"There it is." He says huskily into my ear. "Is that what you want? You want me to kiss you?" he teases as his lips hover over my waiting skin just below my ear.

"Yes." I say breathlessly.

"You want me to kiss you here?" he says as his lips connect with my shoulder, "Or here?" his hand cups my bare pussy, sending a rush of hot need boiling throughout my body.

"Yes" at this point, I should give myself a pat on the back for even managing to squeeze that out. My brain is on fire, as is the rest of my body. All from Gideon's touch alone.

Snow

"Which is it?" I feel his middle finger part my slit and gently rub at the hooded bundle of nerves that lies beneath.

"Yes I want you to kiss me," I take a deep breath as my eyes rolls backwards from his penetrating touch. "I want you kiss me down there." I tug on the arm massaging my clit for emphasis.

"You want me to kiss your pussy, Snow?" he continues to play dumb as my body writhes beneath his magical fingers.

"Yes." I'm a panting mess.

"I'll kiss it, Snow. But first I want to feel what's mine. Not only are you going to come on my face, but I want you right here as well." His hand squeezes my lips and I gasp in surprise. "Spread your legs a little wider for me, baby." his foot comes in practically knocking my feet further apart, leaving me completely exposed to his ravaging hand.

One arm wraps around my chest and slides beneath the cups of my bathing suit top and attaches to my already hardened nipple. The minute his fingers pinch my already sensitive nipple, fireworks begin to explode behind my eyelids. My center floods with my juices soaking his hand completely.

"That's it, Snow. Get nice and wet for me." I feel his middle finger trace around my hole and slowly make its way inside. It feels intrusive at first, but after a few seconds my body relaxes around it.

"Gideon." I moan his name. His finger picks up speed as does the growing feeling inside me. It starts down low, gradually growing larger and larger the more his fingers assault my core. His thumb latches on to my clit, rubbing in furious circles as he inserts another finger into my center. I feel full and satiated all at once.

"Come on Snow, let it go." He urges as he picks up speed. "I want all of you, right now." He commands. In an instant my body convulses around him. One pinch of my nipple sends me flying over the edge. I swear I lose all sense of reality. The only thing keeping me up straight is Gideon's strong hold wrapped around my midsection. I close my eyes for just a second as he runs his hand through my hair.

Snow

"Snow?" I hear his voice from far away. It's a struggle to even open my eyes. "Baby, wake up." I open my eyes and I'm suddenly on the bed.

"What happened?" my voice is husky.

"You had one hell of an orgasm." He chuckles. My cheeks heat up with bright red fire as embarrassment washes over me. "Don't be embarrassed Snow, that was the hottest thing I've ever seen." He tucks a stray hair behind my ear as I bury my head in his chest to hide from humiliation.

"Oh my god." I groan.

"Not god sweetheart, just me." he wiggles his eyebrows and I can't help but laugh.

"That was…" I trail off trying to find the correct phrase.

"Amazing? Exceptional? Extraordinary?" he suggests.

"You're such a pig!" I push against his shoulder rolling out from under him. My legs feel like jelly and my head is still dizzy.

"I wasn't kidding, Snow. You were all of those things." He pins me against the soft mattress, staring deeply into my eyes. "And much, much more." I bring my hands up to either side of his face and bring his mouth towards mine. Our lips erupt in a passionate kiss. His body rests against mine as his groin grinds against my already sensitive core.

"I don't know if I'll be able to stop." He pulls away out of breath.

"So don't." I go for his lips again but he pulls away at the last minute.

"I'm serious Adeline, there's no going back from here. I don't just want half of you. I want all of you, flaws and fucking all." His eyes are dark and stormy.

"I want you too." I practically stutter against his mouth. His lips crash against mine as his large hand wraps around my back pulling at the thin strings of my bikini strap.

"You don't understand, Snow. I don't know if I can take things slow with you." His warning should sound off alarm bells in the back of my head, but nothing seems to be working. I'm more of a rip the band aid off quickly rather than peel it back slowly kind of girl anyway.

Snow

"I don't want slow." I proclaim. "I want fast. I want going over the ledge on the fastest roller coaster, hearts beating in your ass kind of fast." The sound of Gideon's full belly laugh sends trickles of warmth down my spine. I could listen to that sweet sound of dripping honey any day.

"Is your heart beating in your ass now?" he whispers as his fingers pull at the strings of my bikini bottoms. His lips suckle at the skin just above my nipples while his stormy eyes stare holes through me.

"Sort of." I say breathlessly. Gideon falls back on his heels taking my bottoms all the way off. My top was gone a few moments ago, and now I'm completely naked. Somewhere deep down I feel vulnerable, but the aching need inside of me is too strong to care.

"What about now?" he asks as his shorts are removed next. My mouth waters at the length of him. I don't even know how all of that is going to fit inside of me.

"Maybe." I tease. He crawls up my body. Inch by agonizing inch he leaves me breathless.

"And now?" his lips are a hair's breadth away from mine. I close my eyes and give myself the contact I need. This kiss is different. I can feel it from deep down in my bones.

"Yes." A million times yes! My heart has been beating out of my ass since the first time I met Gideon. He's made me nervous, needy, excited, giddy, breathless... He's everything wrapped in one.

"This will hurt." His voice breaks slightly with his warning. I nod in return, watching as he lines his length up against my folds. He slides it back and forth, up and down spreading my wetness all around. My breathing picks up from anticipation. I feel as if it might swallow me.

"I'm a- I've never done this before." I blurt. I feel the embarrassment creep up my neck and onto my cheeks before Gideon can even respond. I sound so stupid I could slap myself.

"I know, Snow." He centers himself as I take a deep breath. "Just relax baby." his words calm me just enough for him to make his grand entrance. I grip onto his shoulders and try to bury my head in his chest. My body feels invaded by him. Inch by inch he pushes in deeper and deeper. The further he goes the more pain I feel, all the way until he presses against my hymen.

"You ready, Snow?" I can barely breathe let alone talk. All I can manage is a weak nod. In one quick thrust he breaks the thin barrier and buries himself deep inside of me. I feel full and a part of me feels as if it's been torn to shreds. It stings mostly, and even more so the faster Gideon seems to move. We stay locked tight for what seems like hours but can only actually be a few minutes. I feel his body relax as he slides out only to thrust back in. I wince on impact but after a few more strokes my body seems to push back.

My teeth bite into the skin on his shoulder as my nails dig into his back. His hips pick up speed as I hang on for dear life. Gideon was right. There was no way he was going to go slow. I don't think he has a slow bone in his body.

"Gideon!" I moan his name. It even surprises me.

"That's it, Snow. I want to hear you scream my name." His hands grab onto my hips as an all too

187

familiar ache starts to build deep inside my core. His pounding is relentless. Each thrust has my body humming with lust and desire.

"Gideon!" This time my voice is louder, as he only seems to spur it on. "Fuck, Gideon." I trail off. It's as if I'm climbing a mountain only to be rewarded once I reach the top. And man do I want that reward.

"Come on baby, give me what I want. Come for me, come all over my dick." His dirty talk turns my cheeks red and my whole entire body seems to blush. I'm so close I can feel it.

"Gideon, I'm coming!" I nearly shout. My legs shake, as my body convulses. My core tightens and begins to pulse around Gideon's thick length. I feel his hot seed fill me to the brim as he collapses completely on top of me. Our breathing is hot and heavy. We're a jumbled mess of naked limbs. It all just feels so natural. When I'm finally able to catch my breath I sigh in contentment.

"Jesus Christ." Gideon mutters as he slides out of me, leaving me feel completely empty. All these years I never knew what I was missing. I feel as if I just gave Gideon the biggest piece of my heart I know I'll never get back. *"Never get attached Adeline."* My mother's words play over and over in the back of mind but I'm afraid it's too late. I think I've already fallen.

"Snow?" Gideon's voice pierces through my reverie and I bring my eyes up to meet his stormy ones. His brow is furrowed. I reach out to trace my finger along the thick patch of hair to smooth it out. He looks so much better when he's relaxed.

"Hmm?" I continue to trace along the contours of his face, memorizing each piece and locking them away in the back of my mind.

"Were you listening?" he asks. He must know by my blank expression that I wasn't paying attention at all. "I asked you if you were alright?" he looks concerned as he searches my eyes for any sign of discontentment.

"I'm fine." I reply. I don't know how to openly tell him exactly how I fell. I feel cherished, free, full...satiated. I'm feeling every single emotion under the sun.

"Are you hurting?" he asks as his lips brush against my temple. The gesture makes my heart turn to mush.

"Just a little sore, I'll be fine." I can tell he's a little worried. It hurt at first; the initial thrust was more shocking than it was painful. Even though I knew what to expect it all still took me by surprise. "Where are you going?" I ask in confusion as Gideon gets up from the bed and begins to dress himself.

"I have to make a phone call." He states firmly. I can't help the way my shoulders slump and my heart aches at his abrupt change. He seems distant. As if his entire mood has shifted in the blink of an eye.

"Okay." I watch as his body retreats from the bedroom, leaving me completely alone.

Chapter 20

Gideon

If I thought I was in trouble before, I'm in even deeper shit now. I promised Ryan over and over again I wouldn't get involved with Adeline and I failed fucking miserably. He said to stay away from her.

He told me to run as far away from her as I could and what did I do? I took her and we ran together. And then I claimed her like a savage beast. I should have never brought her here. I tried like hell to ignore her, thought if I could find odd jobs to do around the house I could keep my mind off of her, but nothing worked. Every single time I saw her pert body in that skimpy bikini all the blood in my body seemed to rush straight to my dick. I told myself over and over that I wouldn't take her, that stealing kisses every now and then was enough. But it wasn't.

First I claimed her with my mouth. Then I watched in awe as she fell apart against my fingers. When I finally sank my dick so deep inside of her I damn near had a heart attack. Leaving her in the bed we just fucked like wild animals in was painful for her and for me. As soon as I looked in her sea blue eyes, I felt an incredible amount of guilt. I took her when I shouldn't have; it's just going to make things worse for her in the end.

"Hello?" Ryan's gruff voice answers the phone on the other end as I step outside. The warm sea breeze sends the salty air my way invading my nostrils as I inhale deeply.

"I fucked up." I run a frustrated hand through my hair.

"You fucked her didn't you?" I can almost see the disappointment on his face as his voice comes through the phone.

Snow

"I didn't mean too." I lie. "I mean... Jesus fuck did I fuck up." I hear him chuckle in the background before he tries to cover it up.

"Come on Gideon, how many times did I tell you to stay away from her?" I pinch the bridge of my nose as I try to think of a way to dig myself out of this massive hole. "Bowler is going to flip his fucking lid."

"I know he is." I say in a panic. "I don't know what came over me!"

"I know what came over you Gideon. You took a young woman to your fucking beach house thinking you weren't going to fuck her. You stupidly thought having a young woman whore around in a goddamn bikini wasn't going to get your dick constantly hard." I can feel his anger through the phone.

"She didn't whore around." I try to defend her but it's no use.

"I told you to end things before they got too far and you completely fucked everything up. Bowler is going to flip, and the whole operation could be in the shitter now."

"I told you she doesn't know anything about that."

"No, what you told me was that girl has a whole bunch of mommy and daddy issues. Don't let her play the damsel in distress, you're just going to let yourself get fooled." He keeps talking over me every time I try to butt in.

"That's not what I said, Ryan. I told you everything she told me. Every single fucking thing. I'm telling you she has no fucking clue her momma's supplying half of the east coast with grade A meth." I practically shout. I move further away from the house so there's no chance of Adeline hearing our conversation.

"And I'm telling you she's lying. There ain't no goddamn way she can live in the same house all these years with the biggest lab sitting smack dab under her nose." I hear him inhale deeply. "You're in some serious shit Gideon. I bailed you out so many times when we were in Iraq, but I don't think I can help you this time." He sounds defeated.

Snow

"Just tell Bowler to hold off a little longer, I'll try to get more info." I know I'm making empty promises. I'm only trying to buy Adeline more time, and buy us more time together.

"That's not possible Gideon; Bowler says he wants to move in on Monday. As of yesterday he still wanted you leading everything." Fuck. I'm in deep shit.

"But Monday's only four days away, that's too soon."

"Monday is it Gideon. Make sure you get rid of the girl before then. If Bowler, and that's a big if, still wants you on this case make sure you're prepared for it. Don't let any feelings get in the way of the career you've been working your whole life for." I sigh in defeat. Ryan's right, I shouldn't have put everything in jeopardy.

"Yeah, okay." I reply before hanging up. How the hell am I supposed to get rid of Adeline in just a few days? We were supposed to stay here for at least another week.

"Gideon?" I whip my head around and come face to face with a blushing Adeline... my Snow. "Is everything alright?" she asks. Her body gives away all her true feelings, and right now I can see how worried she is. "I thought I heard yelling." Her cute brows furrow into worry lines across her forehead.

"Everything's fine, Snow. I was just on the phone with my boss." I take a deep breath. "Looks like we have to cut this little vacation short, somethings come up at work." I look away from her, not wanting to see the disappointment written across her beautiful face.

"When do we leave?" she asks.

"Tonight." I walk by her swiftly, leaving her at the end of the driveway all by herself. Everything will be easier to deal with if I keep my distance. For the both of us.

Chapter 21

Adeline

When I heard his raised voice seeping through the opened window, I decided to go outside to investigate it. I caught the last of Gideon's conversation, and from the looks of it, it was not a nice one. Gideon's hair was mussed as if he ran his hand through it a thousand times out of frustration, whoever he was speaking to just completely ruined everything. Not only that, but Gideon seems angry...at me.

We pack our bags in silence. The awkward tension threatening to pull me under like the oceans waves outside. Gideon's tense. His shoulders are stiff and he hasn't said a word to me. Max sits at my heels as

I move from drawer to drawer collecting what little things I brought. Everything fits into my ratty backpack and I'm ready in just a few minutes.

"Why don't you take Max out to the truck while I lock up?" He doesn't even look at me, but I nod to him anyway. I walk with Max out to the big truck, the whole time thinking of what went wrong. What did I do to make him like this? Maybe he saw what I was feeling. Maybe he thinks I'll get too attached. The sad part is I'm afraid he's right.

"What's his problem boy?" Max grumbles besides me. We wait only a few minutes for Gideon to get into the truck. I watch with sadness as we reverse down the driveway, leaving behind the only piece of paradise I've ever known. I feel that I'm leaving my heart behind. The car ride is long and silent. You could cut the tension in the cab with a knife. The only time we stop is to let Max out to use the bathroom.

Gideon spends the whole ride giving me the silent treatment. His silence makes me feel as if I made a mistake. Crossing the line from friends to lovers had to of been a bad idea, if that's what's causing his sour attitude. I thought things were going good, but now I'm left with all of this confusion.

When we pull into the driveway to my house my heart sinks. I don't want to be here. I want to be back at the beach, with the sand caked in my hair and sun burning me to a crisp. I want fluffy blankets and Gideon as my safety net. I don't want to walk into my bedroom and remember my life is nothing but trash. I don't want to walk into that house and be reminded I'm never going to get out. A part of me wishes I never saw that other side. The grass was greener, but this brown is all I'll ever know.

"I'll call you." Gideon states, but I don't believe him. I try desperately to contain the sting of the tears threatening to escape. I nod in response, give Max a kiss on the head and hop down from the truck. I don't turn around as he backs down the driveway. I just continue forward with my shitty backpack to my shitty house.

The windows and doors are completely open. All the curtains seem to have been removed and the house reeks of the most putrid odor.

"Where the hell have you been?" I stop in the kitchen doorway and come face to face with my mother. She looks as if she's lost ten pounds in one week I've been gone. Her hair is going crazy and her eyes are sunken in with dark bags underneath.

"I was at Tim's." I lie. She looks at me as if she doesn't believe me, when she's never questioned me before.

"That's not what Todd said. He told me you went off with your new boyfriend."

"How would he know? He's never met Tim, and I don't have a boyfriend." Technically it's not a lie.

"Are you lying?" she asks. I look at her as if she's grown ten heads. Is this woman serious?

"Does it matter? Why the sudden interest in my life?" I go into the fridge to search for a bottle of water and come up empty handed.

"I don't need any strangers knowing anything about us Adeline, it's bad enough with all the rumors I don't need you starting more." *What the hell?*

"What the hell does that mean?" she steps towards me with a bony finger pushing into my chest.

Snow

"All I'm saying Adeline, is that when you say you're with Tim, you better be with Tim." Looking into her rabid eyes I can see she's completely wired out. Her new hubby must be supplying her with all she needs to get high. She looks panicked and paranoid. For a second it makes me worried. *What the hell is with everyone today?*

"Fine." I leave it at that. I walk away before things get even weirder. When I'm finally in the comfort of my own room I can breathe. Everything looks to be in place. The booby traps I set are still in place, not that I have anything valuable in here to steal anyway.

It's already past eight o'clock, and after the day I've had I feel utterly exhausted. I'm still a little sore from earlier. Thinking back on everything now it all seems like it happened years ago. I can't say that it didn't hurt like hell to have Gideon completely switch gears on me. Getting the silent treatment after handing over every single piece of my heart and body, made my heart ache and my eyes sting.

All these years I've never let someone get as close to me as Gideon did. I knew better than to trust someone I barely know. I've seen my mother's feelings get crushed over and over again by guy after guy, and yet I went and did the same exact thing. Something about Gideon seemed different...trustworthy. He said he'd call, but even I know that was a bold faced lie.

All these thoughts run rampant through my mind as I try to fall asleep. I analyze every word, every smile every movement. After a while I finally manage to fall asleep with the image of Gideon's smiling face floating through my mind.

Snow

Chapter 22

Adeline

"You got a hot date or something?" Jake asks. We're all sitting around our table on Tim's back deck.

"What?" I ask in confusion. I watch as he passes a joint to Tim and my throat goes dry. Gideon once told me I was better than that, better than the rumors that follow me around so I've been trying the sober route, even though right now I'm dying for a high.

"You haven't stopped looking at your phone since you got here Add's." He lets out a puff of smoke. I pry my eyes away from my phone and decide to tuck it back into my pocket. It's been a few days now with no word at all. If he hasn't said anything by now I doubt he'll say anything at all.

"My mom was supposed to send me a list of shit to get from the store." I shrug my shoulders. I see Tim's eyes zero in on me as if he knows its bullshit. I hear him mumble something but decide to let it go. My eyes drift next-door. The lights are off and the curtains are closed, the house is eerily quiet. My heart hurts thinking about Max. He must be sad all by himself. For a little while we were buddies. He was like my little sidekick.

"Addy?" I turn my head back towards to the boys.

"What?"

"You want some?" Jake holds the joint in my direction and I'm tempted to take it.

"No I'm good; I'm not feeling too hot." What I can't say is that I'm dying from a broken heart. My stomach aches and the empty feeling in my chest seems to grow bigger and bigger by the day.

Snow

"You alright?" Tim asks. I make contact with his eyes and see the underlying meaning. I shake my head and I see his withdraw slightly.

"I'm good, just probably going to head home soon." I wait around for as long as I can, hoping to catch a glimpse of the recluse next door. Only he wasn't a recluse, he was my friend. In the end I thought we could be more. You read about summer romance and watch it on TV, and only if you're lucky you get to experience it for yourself. Mine was short lived and was anything but a romance, but it was a whirlwind of emotions all mixed in one even if they were one sided.

"You want us to walk you?" Tim asks.

"Nah, I'll be good." I stand on tired legs and say my goodbyes. It feels weird leaving with a clear mind on steady feet.

When I get to my driveway I notice an all-black SUV sitting by the mailbox. The windows are tinted, probably illegally and there's not even a license plate. I continue to walk wearily by, but the hairs on the back of my neck stand up anyway.

"Ma?" I yell when I come through the door. I go to the kitchen in search of her and find the basement door open. "Ma?" I take a step down and listen. I hear my mom and Todd speaking in hushed whispers. I continue to take each step carrying me further and further into the basement. My heart beats like a drum. Todd's warning to stay away runs through the back of my mind.

When I get onto the bottom step I gasp. It looks as if they made the entire basement into a kitchen. Glass beakers and bottles sit atop burners. Propane tanks with rubber tubes running into large clear jugs line the floor. The walls are stained yellow and the chemical odor is overwhelming.

"What the fuck are you doing down here?" Todd bellows from somewhere in the basement.

"What is this?" I yell when my mother's small form stands before me. She's in nothing but her underwear.

"Go back upstairs Adeline!" she yells. When I don't follow her orders I feel Todd's hand grip into my bicep and start to lug me up the stairs one by one.

Snow

"Let go of me!" I screech. I scratch and claw away at his hand but it's no use. He throws me into the counter when we finally make it back into the kitchen. I hit my side so hard it knocks the wind out of me.

"She told you not to go down there!" he bellows into my face. Spittle fly's against my skin like little pins.

"What the fuck is that?" I back up putting enough distance between me and the burly man. "What are you, fucking cookers?" my heart is pounding out of my chest as I realize I just saw something I shouldn't have. Jesus fucking Christ I'm in deep shit.

"You ruined everything!" Todd yells. His face is red and smoke is practically pouring out of his ears. My mother suddenly appears at his side. She looks worried and panicked.

"Mom, is this what you've been doing?" I ask her in disbelief. "You've been using our fucking house as a goddamn lab?" I scream. My cheeks are so red they're on fire. I'm so incredibly angry I could boil over. I know enough to know exactly what that was. I've lived on the shitty side of town all my life, everyone around here

207

knows what a goddamn lab looks like. I can't understand why I didn't see it sooner, the smell, the trash, the open windows and no curtains. How did I not recognize all the signs?

"Calm down, Adeline!" she scolds me as if I'm a little child throwing a temper tantrum. *How fucking dare she!*

"Calm down? Did you seriously just fucking say that?" I need to get out of here before I have a full blown panic attack. I need Jaimie, no... I need Gideon. I make a run from the kitchen with my mom calling after me. As soon as I run through the front door I run into a massive wall. I fall backwards landing hard on my ass. As if it's the straw that broke the camel's back, the flood gates finally break loose.

"Gideon?" I ask astonished as I look up. He's standing above me with a black uniform on, a small gun gripped tightly in his left hand. "What are you doing here?" I ask.

"Adeline, what are you doing here? You were supposed to be at Tim's!" he practically bellows. He moves just and inch and the word Detective reads loud

208

and clear across the front of his uniform. My eyebrows crunch together in confusion.

"What are you wearing?" my mind can't seem to comprehend what's directly in front of me.

"I'm sorry, but you weren't supposed to be here." He whispers for only me to hear. "I have one suspect over here!" he yells. As soon as the words leave his mouth a line of black uniforms swarm my house and yard. Gideon stands me up and turns me around. As he takes both of my wrists from behind I can hear him reciting words to me. I'm still too confused to understand anything. *Am I being arrested?" What is this?*

"Gideon, what's going on?" I ask as he pushes me towards a blue and white cruiser.

"You have the right to remain silent, anything you say may be used against you in a court of law." As if it's all finally sinking in now I start to panic.

"I didn't do anything!" I try to wriggle away. "Gideon I didn't do anything!" my voice grows louder the closer we get to the cruiser. Somewhere in the background I can hear my mother and Todd yelling.

"Just cooperate, Adeline. Everything will be fine, I promise." He whispers into my ear. My body goes into fight or flight mode and I do anything but cooperate. I struggle to break out of his hold and in the midst of the altercation about three other large guys come running over.

"Please!" I yell. "I didn't do anything, please just let me go!" Two huge men come forward and grip each of my biceps. Gideon steps away, leaving me in the hands of these beasts. I watch as he makes his way towards the house. "Gideon! Tell them, tell them I didn't do anything!" I plead with him to help me but he turns his head away. I swear to god my heart breaks on impact and I'm left a sobbing mess.

I'm lead to a small police cruiser with thing one and thing two holding onto me for dear life. The cab of the small car is dark and dingy, and smells like stale air.

"Where are you taking me?" I ask for the millionth time in the past thirty seconds. "I didn't do anything." I swear the officer in front of me just smirks as he drives down the street, leaving all traces of commotion fast behind us. All the way to the police station I try to reason with the officer in the front seat but my pleas fall on deaf ears. My wrists sting and my eyes are red and swollen. Just a few hours ago I was enjoying the company of my two best friends, thinking the worst thing in life was Gideon ignoring me. *How wrong was I!*

When we finally get to the station, it's not just any police station it's the state police barracks. My heart sinks as I'm pulled from the back seat and forced to walk towards the building. People stare with disapproving eyes. Other officers I saw at my house line the steps with looks of approval as I'm brought inside. I make eye contact with the darkest pair of chocolate brown eyes I've ever seen and try to convey the amount of hatred I feel for him.

Gideon's a detective. He must have used me to gain information on my mom and her husband. It all makes sense now. I was nothing put a pawn for him to manipulate and play with for the time being. All of our late night conversations, jokes, and kisses meant nothing to him. I meant nothing to him.

I'm placed in a cold room, and left all alone. I can't help the traitorous tears that slip down my cheeks every now and again as I allow myself to feel sorry for myself. My throat is sore, my cheeks are puffy and my ears are red and burning. I sit on the cold metal bench and bring my knees up to my chest. My hands are still cuffed behind my back which makes any position uncomfortable. I lay my head on my knees and wait in agony for someone to come and get me out of here.

Snow

Chapter 23

Gideon

"I told you she had nothing to do with this!" I pace back and forth in Bowlers office as Ryan watches on from behind me. "Name one fucking piece of evidence you have against her besides the fact that she's related to that scumbag!" I am so angry. The way they treated Snow like she was a criminal made me infuriated. The way I treated her was awful, and I have no doubt she'll ever want to speak to me again.

Bowler sits at his desk with his hands in a steeple, staring at me as I go off in front of him.

"I told you time and time again, there was no need to have her on your goddamn suspect list, but this whole time you insisted. Now look, you have an innocent scared woman sitting in a cold cell who has no fucking clue about what's going on!" I'm practically growling as I speak. My chest is heaving with frustration.

"Are you done, Gideon?" Bowler asks calmly.

"No I'm not done; I won't be done until you have her out of this goddamn place." Ryan shoots me a warning glare from the side, no doubt worried I'm going to set off the big cheese.

"As soon as my guys take her in for questioning, and she passes she'll be free to go." He speaks calmly, when I'm anything but.

"Don't you have enough evidence already? Her mother and that bastard both said she had no idea what was going on!"

"Is there a reason why you're sticking your neck out for this woman more than you normally would?" he questions. I know he already knows. Ryan has one hell of a big mouth. There's no way he hasn't said anything about my relationship with the woman in question.

Snow

"I just think that someone who's so blatantly innocent shouldn't be kept overnight for the fun of it."

"It's not for fun, Gideon. Its protocol." He scolds as he stands from his chair. "I told you not to get involved with anyone, warned you about what would happen, and yet you went and done it anyway!" he yells in my face as he towers over me. "I never told you to go out and fuck the suspect, I told you to watch her. It took what?" he looks over to Ryan, "One day to fuck everything up?" he chastises me. "You're one lucky son of a bitch I don't dock your pay and send you home on leave! Now get the hell out of my office. Your girlfriend will be out in the morning!" he points an angry finger at the door. He doesn't have to tell me twice.

I head to the place I know they're keeping Adeline... the holding cell. When I peek through the small window I can see Snow's small form huddled on the small metal bench. She looks lost, lonely, and incredibly sad. My heart hurts seeing her in there. She'll never know how hard I tried to keep her out of this place.

215

I spent months watching her and her friends, and it took only a short amount of time to fall in love with her. She looks as broken now as she did when I first found her. She was broken, but I've slowly watched her crawl her way out of that dark place only to be thrown back there once again.

Against better judgment I take my keys out and make my way into the tiny cell. I can hear her quiet sniffles as soon as step foot inside.

"Snow?" I whisper. Her head snaps up, her eyes searing with pain and anger. I go to kneel before her and she scoots away. Her arms are still wrenched behind her and I grab for my keys. I reach for her but she moves once again. "Hold still, I'm just trying to unlock you." I jiggle the keys in front of her and her eyes wearily search mine. She seems incredibly skittish and withdrawn. I grab hold of the cuff and put the key in. As soon as her arms slip free they fall to her sides. She's been in this cell for hours, her arms must be numb. "It helps if you shake them out." I say to her. She tucks them into herself and hovers into the far corner. I go to sit by her and begin to speak.

216

Snow

"I don't want to speak to you." She snaps. I can't say it doesn't hurt, because it does...immensely.

"I just want to make sure you're alright." I feel as if I'm speaking to a wall. She does everything she can to avoid me.

"Please just go away, Gideon." The way she says my name makes my heart shatter. The guilt I had before threatens to consume me when I think about all the ways I've betrayed her.

"They said you'll be out of here in the morning." I try once more but even I know I sound like an asshole.

"I don't want to speak to you anymore, please leave me alone." her eyes meet mine and I can feel the hatred rolling off of her in waves. I get up to leave and make my way towards the door.

"I'm sorry." I tell her just before I leave the room.

Chapter 24

Adeline

It feels as if I've spent hours and hours in questioning. Over and over again Detective Ryan asks me the same exact questions. I told him everything I knew right down to the discovery in the basement. He watches me as if he thinks I'm lying. For once in my life I'm not.

The only reason I have some leverage right now is because Gideon paid for my lawyer, and he's not the cheap court appointed kind. As much as I didn't want to accept it I didn't really have much of a choice. At some point they told me my mother confessed to everything, including my innocence. So even though things seem to be looking up, I still feel incredibly broken.

I still feel insecure as I walk out of the police station doors. A million judgmental eyes follow me all the way to the small car parked along the curb. When they told me I could make a phone call the first face that popped up in my mind was Gideon. As much as my heart hurts, I can't seem to relay the message to my already confused brain.

I can't seem to get the image of everything out of my head. The way Gideon just left me. The way I yelled for him, finally allowing myself to need someone as much as I needed him in that moment. Watching him walk away and taking every single piece of my heart with him. I guess I didn't realize how attached I had grown. I guess the saying never put all of your eggs in one basket is true. In this case my eggs were my feelings.

Throughout the night Gideon kept coming in to check on me. By the last time he came in I was so consumed with anger all I wanted to do was slap him. The way he spoke so gently made me want to curl up in his lap and cry, while also making me want to scream in his face and rip his eyes out. How could I seriously feel so back and forth on this?

On more than one occasion he whispered how sorry he was. For a moment or two I almost believed him, until I read the shiny silver badge that read Detective Wellfleet right across the front of his chest. It was just a constant reminder of how wrong I was about him.

I know he used me like yesterday's trash. Unlike me he was taking the voluntary information I was giving him and storing it away for a whole other reason. While I placed and packaged each and every word and memory in the back of my head, he was calculating and manipulating me to give up more. *How could I have been so blind?*

Not many times did my mind drift away to my mother. *Was she at the same station as me? Is she in the cell next door?*

My mind raced with all the possibilities. For a while I didn't know if I was ever going to be able to leave. Part of the deal for being let go was having absolutely no contact with my mother. Luckily for me that's going to be much easier than I thought. According to Detective Ryan, she's going to be away for a very long time.

Apparently for the last year and a half my mother has been running one of the biggest lab operations in all of Massachusetts. All of which was done right out of our basement. I spent so much of the past two years in such a haze I never saw what was right in front of me. I grew up with my mother constantly high with a new man every other day. I should have seen the signs. When I think about all of them now I can see everything so clearly. The whole marriage to Todd was also a ruse. Apparently they had been working together for months. What I can't see so clearly is from where my mother went from drug user to drug lord. It doesn't make any sense. How can someone jump so far one way?

What Detective Ryan also told me was that even though I'd be leaving here today, I wouldn't have a home to go back to. The whole property is a crime scene and everything inside of the house has been labeled contaminated. Everything I owned is essentially gone.

One minute I'm lounging on a beautiful beach with a brand new bikini and the next I'm walking out of the state police barracks with nothing left but the clothes on my back.

The sun outside is incredibly bright and does nothing to soothe my pounding headache. The air is warm and stuffy for a midsummer morning. I stretch my legs and reach my arms out, letting out a ginormous yawn.

"Snow!" I hear his voice but force myself to continue walking. "Adeline, wait!" Gideon grabs my arm as I spin around and slap him as hard as I can. My hand flies up to my mouth as I realize what I just did.

"I...I" I stutter trying to come up with an apology my mouth can't seem to produce.

"I deserved that." Gideon shocks me as the words fall from his mouth. "I deserve everything you hit me with. I didn't want any of this to end up like this." His eyes search mine for something I know I'm incapable of at this moment.

Snow

Forgiveness.

Time seems to stand still as I stare into his dark brown eyes. A car horn goes off in the distance, a woman yells, and a baby starts to cry. The world around me seems to keep spinning as mine comes to a standstill.

"Say something." He pleads. As if his words have slapped me back to reality I finally find my bearings.

"I hate you." I wrench my arm away from his grasp as his shoulders slump. I leave him standing there like a statue as I make my way to the little red car waiting for me. I force myself not to look back as we pull away.

"Are you ready?" Jaimie looks at me from the driver's seat.

"As I'll ever be." He pats my knee with his big hand. The spark that used to be there whenever he touched me is long gone. Gone are the feelings of something more. I love Jaimie, but after loving Gideon for as shortly as I did I know it's not the forever kind.

Building by building, street by street, tree by tree I watch my whole world pass me by. I feel a sense of normalcy with Jaimie sitting beside me, and the wind blowing against my face. The further we get, the further my past can stay behind me. I won't stop until it's completely gone, until each and every memory fades in the distance.

Chapter 25

Letter #1

Snow,

I don't know where to begin. Should I go back to that first day I agreed to take on the case against your mother or go back to the first night I found you in my yard? It all just seems so far away, irrelevant towards the feelings I have for you now.

I'm not sure where it all went wrong, or when those feelings switched from doing my civil duty, to loving the woman I knew I was going to ruin. I let things get so far. I almost believed that none of it existed. That being with you made me forget it was all a ruse.

I fought for you, in the end. I knew you were innocent. All it took was one look at you and I knew. I tried hard, to let none of this shit even get to you but I managed to fuck it up anyway. It took all but one summer to completely throw everything I ever knew directly out the window. The minute I looked into your tortured eyes I was a goner. You're the only woman I know who can bring me to my damn knees, and lift me higher than the sky within the same breath. I feel like a damn pansy, writing you this letter. But I need you to know. Know that I love you, and know that I understand why you left. I know it's easier to move on once you put about a thousand miles of distance between you and me. Is it normal to suddenly feel so lost an empty?

P.S Max is a sad sack of shit without you. I've never seen him so depressed. He misses you.

-Gideon

Chapter 26

Letter #23

Snow,

I dreamt about you last night, it was so real. The way your skin felt against mine. The way you lit up from head to toe when I ran my fingers over your smooth pale skin. I couldn't sleep after that. Pictures of you ran rampant through my mind for hours. That mixed with Max's constant whimpering managed to keep me up the rest of the night.

Bowler has me doing a desk job. Apparently too much was compromised last time, and they don't want to risk it again. What he doesn't understand is that there's only one woman in this whole fucking world I'd risk it all for. You. They don't understand how caged in this tiny cubicle actually makes me feel. Hell I don't even remember the last time I felt anything.

I went to the beach house, it needed to be winterized. Massachusetts winters really give it a beating each year. I swear it still smelt like you. I could practically feel your presence there with me, wished for you to be with me. It felt wrong to be there...without you. Like it does each and every day we're apart. It fucking sucks. Everything does.

-Gideon

Snow

Chapter 27

Letter #46

Snow,

The days are getting shorter and the winter air has completely taken over. The soft snowflakes cover the ground like a blanket, reminding me of you, Snow.

I quit my job...sort of. I still do random jobs for Ryan when he needs it.

I still miss you, as always. It gets harder and harder to send these letters, knowing every time there will never be a reply. I still had your number in my phone, until the last time I called it said it was disconnected. I can take the hint. I'm slowly waiting for the day my letters get forwarded back to me. It hasn't happened yet so for now I'll keep writing. In all of my fucked up misery it's the only thing I can still manage to hang onto. I never knew I was a writer until this, until you. Besides the whiskey, this seems to be my only escape.

I have close to nothing left. No job, no family, no...you. It's strange when I think about how fast you were able to worm your way into my heart. How the steel walls around my heart slowly turned to mush whenever you were around. It's true. Why else would I be sitting here writing these letters like a love struck girl?

P.S Max told me he missed you, or maybe that was just my drunken mind playing tricks again.

-Gideon

Chapter 28

Letter #98

Snow,

I think this is it. The last letter I'll write at least for now. I hope you found everything you are looking for. I hope I didn't manage to mess your life up too badly. I know you went to Alabama to start over, exactly what you should have done.

You deserve everything I should have given you. You deserve the trust and love I know you can find within someone else. I deserve my misery. I deserve the hole I dug for myself.

People always thought I was crazy before, they have no fucking clue now. Thank fuck for the wonders of amazon and everything to do with online ordering. I swear I haven't left this goddamn house in months. In order to move on with my life I'm forcing myself to give up on these...on you. It's better for both of us. I'm fucking sorry I dragged it out for so goddamn long in the first place. I won't forget it, and I definitely won't regret it. So I guess this is goodbye. At least until I'm an emotional drunken mess and decide to write to you yet again. I make no promises.

P.S I've been telling Max you still love him, I think it makes him feel better. He still whines and whimpers but I think he's getting better.

P.P.S I love you Snow.

-Gideon

Chapter 29

Gideon

"Get up! I'm not going to sit here and watch you drink self stupid again." Ryan's fuzzy form comes to stand before me as I lift the glass to my lips and take another swig. The whiskey burns all the way down, scorching my insides and settling deep down into the pit of my stomach.

"So don't." I bite out. "I'm good." I mumble. I empty the rest of the whiskey into my throat and stand up in search for more.

"Come on, Gideon. At the rate you're going you'll be dead in a few months." Ryan grips onto my arm as I stumble before him. "Sit the hell down and get a fucking grip. It's been months Gideon, either man up and get your fucking girl or get the fuck over it." He huffs out a breath and leaves his hands placed firmly on his hips.

"I am over it!" I yell. "I've been over it!" sort of.

"Really?" he questions.

"Yes." I state firmly. I know he can see right through me though, which is why we're currently having this conversation.

"Cause it looks like you're trying to drown self in whiskey. Shit Gideon, Bowlers been on your ass for months and yet all you do is throw back tumblers of whiskey. When you going to give it up?" he eyes me up and down. I hate how he knows exactly how I'm feeling or thinking. "You quit your fucking job, and you've resulted to drowning yourself in whiskey for the past however many months. When was the last time you even left the house, to mail another letter?" I try to block out his incessant talking but it does no use. His throaty voice pierces through my walls making me more annoyed and angry by the minute.

"I stopped being Bowlers bitch the moment he pulled that shit with me." My confession makes his eyes widen. "I won't ever do it again."

"You don't mean that man. You worked your whole goddamn life for this spot. I can't believe you just gave it all up." He tries to bargain with my thoughts but it's no use. Nothing I do can escape the guilt I feel or the loneliness that invades my bones. Adeline came into my life for the shortest amount of time and yet she made the biggest impact. All the texts, phone calls, and letters I've written have gone unanswered.

"What's it for? Seriously, Ryan. Why the fuck did I work so hard to end up with absolutely nothing?" Max makes a soft noise for somewhere in the room. The damn dog always seems to be talking back to me.

"It's not nothing. This was your life before she came along." He bites out. Obviously the end of his rope is wearing thin.

"You don't fucking get it, no one gets it." I say defeated. As much as I try I know I'll never be able to make things right again.

I watched Adeline leave the station and head towards that beat up little red car. I tried to stop her, one last time to apologize, to beg for forgiveness. But she was having none of it. So I let her walk away from me. I made a choice to watch as she climbed into the passenger seat of Jaimie Hillborn's vehicle. After everything went down Bowler had me put on desk arrest. Meaning the only job I was going to be doing for the next year was paperwork, which lasted for about a week until I quit... for good. So not only did I essentially lose my girl but I lost my job in all sense of the word. Most of my career I've spent out on the battlefield, what's the point of doing it anymore when you're stuck in a cubicle sorting paperwork?

It's been months since Adeline walked away, five to be exact. Every single day since then I've been slowly drowning in my sorrows. I've written her a letter every day of the week since she left. I think I've apologized at least a thousand times in all of them.

"I get it alright. That girl had you whipped from the minute you met her. You think I don't know what it feels like to be completely consumed by someone and then have it all crashing down around you?" I know Ryan had a wife before his most recent one, and I know she was in some kind of accident. But the womanizing Ryan I know would never be capable of what I felt for Adeline would he? "You're not the only one whose loved and lost someone." I place my head in my hands.

"I love her." I admit for the first time. I never even had the chance to tell Adeline before everything went down. But I've written it in almost every letter since.

"You need to go get her and bring her back. Get your head out of your ass and be a goddamn man." He slaps me on the back and stands to leave.

"Where are you going?" I ask as I watch him walk away from me.

"I got a hot date at the bar, and you have somewhere to be. I figured I'd make my departure early." he shrugs and walks out of my house. As much as I hate to admit it Ryan's right. I just don't understand why I waited so long to realize it. "If I come back here and you're still here, I'm going to knock your ass out." he states firmly before closing the door behind him.

Max comes over and rests his head on my knees. His eyes burn a hole through my head as he stares at me.

"What?" I ask him. His eyes perk up and he lets out a howl. "I can't just go get her, it's more complicated than that." If Snow was here right now she'd laugh at the one sided conversation I'm having. He lets out a howl and this time he doesn't stop.

"Okay!" I shout. I get up to my feet and he stays directly by my side. I grab for the keys by the door. "Let's go get our girl back."

Snow

Chapter 30

Adeline

"Mail's here." Jaimie walks into the small apartment with a stack of envelopes tucked under his arm.

"Anything for me?" I have a sliver of hope that maybe Gideon sent me another letter. It's been a few weeks and I can't deny how disappointed I feel. As much as I thought I hated him after everything he put me through, a part of me still loves him. That part of me is still holding on to the thought of him and I being together again. No matter how much I try to tell myself it's over, my heart just won't accept it.

"Yes, another letter from you know who."
Jaimie hands me a tiny envelope as a disapproving look falls across his face.

"It's just a letter Jaimie." I roll my eyes and grab for my keys hanging on the wall beside the door.

"It's never just a letter Adeline. Every time you receive one of those you get all depressed and can barely eat for weeks at a time. It's not good for you and..." he can't say it. He never can.

"I know you're just looking out for me, but I'm a big girl Jaimie, you have to let me make my own decisions." I walk up to him and kiss his cheek softly.

"You want me to go with you?" he asks.

"No, I think I'll be good. Besides I don't want you missing another class for me."

"You sure?" he looks concerned as I take a step out of the door.

"I'm sure Jaimie, I'll be back later." With that I leave.

As I walk through the park I wipe the sweat from my brow and push my hair back. I've been in Alabama for months now and yet I still can't get used to

Snow

the heat. It's mid-winter and yet there's not a snowflake in sight or a temperature below seventy. I'm secretly dying for a Massachusetts blizzard right about now.

I moved down here with Jaimie as soon as he picked me up all those months ago. He's been a complete godsend. I needed an escape and he provided the perfect one. His apartment is tiny and claustrophobic, but his lumpy old couch is all I can afford right now. He doesn't mind me crashing until I can move out on my own. But even though I left that place and time behind me doesn't mean it doesn't show up on my doorstep once a week in the form of a tiny folded up letter, or at least it used too.

Gideon writes me every week. And as much as I shouldn't, I read and re-read each and every single one. I come to the park to read them in private. My surroundings grant me a sort of quiet reprieve and I'm thankful for it.

I haven't spoken to him at all and yet a part of me is still desperately attached to him. I secretly can't wait to receive his letters. I've saved and stored each and every one. Sometimes he still apologizes, and sometimes he'll tell me about Max.

He also took the time to explain to me about my mother's case. He made it much easier to understand all the legal terms my lawyer always used. From what I've read, with all the evidence against my mother and Todd they're facing a crap ton of jail time. But what I long for most are the tiny details he'll slip in about himself.

As I sit down against my favorite oak tree I pull the newest letter from my purse and tear it open. I stare at the words over and over. As if the longer I stare the four words on the page will make more sense.

Snow,
I'm coming for you.
-Gideon

My eyebrows scrunch together in confusion. What the hell does he even mean? The words pop off the page and pierce my heart. After months of feeling nothing, my heart suddenly flutters to life. The words repeat in my head over and over again. He told me the last time was the last time, that there would be no more letters after that.

I'm coming for you. I'm coming for you. I'm coming for you.

The words jump out at me, and crawl all over my skin. I feel them invade my bloodstream and make me go dizzy. *What the hell could he even mean?*

"Adeline." His voice pierces the air around me as I snap my eyes up to meet his. My throat suddenly goes dry. All I manage to do is stare at him. My heart pounds in my chest a mile a minute.

Gideon looks like a god standing before me. His cheeks are covered in a weeks' worth of stubble, making his jawline seem much more prominent. His hair is slightly longer and falling every which way. It looks as if he's grown a foot or two, but I know that's impossible.

His eyes capture me completely. They're tired and anxious all mixed in one. I can see the battle he's fighting within himself. His hands are tucked into his

243

jeans pockets. Part of me wants to run directly into his arms while the other part wants to run for the hills.

"Gideon." His name falls off my lips in a broken whisper.

I'm coming for you.

"What are you doing here?" I ask sheepishly. The way he looks me up and down I can't help but blush. I feel the redness creep up my chest and cheeks. My hands cover my belly in an attempt to hide my growing bump. Thank god I decided to wear an oversized T-Shirt.

"Did you get my last letter?" he asks huskily. I can only manage to nod in response. "Did you read it?" he asks again. My fingertips tighten around the edge of the paper when his eyes zero in on the letter in my lap.

"Yes." I nod my head.

"Then you should know." He takes a step towards me. I stand up with my weight against the tree, using its strength as support.

"Know what?" I whisper, completely mesmerized.

Snow

"That I was coming for you." He takes another step, and then another, and another until he's standing only inches away from me.

I'm coming for you.

I replay the words over and over again.

"Why?" I ask. My eyes zero in on his lips and I can't help the ache that forms deep down in my belly.

"Because I love you, Snow." Inhale. "I should have told you that before things got so fucking complicated." There he is, my Gideon. I knew this uneasy man standing before me was just masking the beast that the lies within. "God I fucked things up so badly." His arm comes out and rests against the tree by my head. His chest is centimeters from my own. He's so close. Any closer and I swear he'd be able to hear my racing heart, or worse find the secret I've been hiding underneath my shirt.

"Gideon... I" His other hand reaches forward to land on my hip as his mouth comes down to meet mine. Out of all of the scenarios that went through my head, seeing Gideon like this wasn't one of them. I've been back and forth on calling him. Whenever I was at my

245

lowest low I'd reach for the phone until Jaimie talked me out of it. It got to the point where I had to block his number completely, to avoid temptation.

"Wait!" I push against his chest the moment his lips reach mine. A small panic attack threatens to make my heart jump out of my butt.

"What's wrong?" he pulls away with his brows pinched together. His eyes travel down my body right to where my hand rests against my stomach. "What are you hiding?" he goes to remove my hand but I shrink away.

"I..." I'm at a loss for words. How do I tell the only man I ever loved that I'm having his baby? After all he did to me? After I ran as far away from him as I possibly could? I feel his fingers lift my shirt as his eyes widen in shock.

"Shit, you're..."

"Pregnant." I force the word past the ball of cotton lodged in my throat. I glance away as my cheeks alight with fire.

"But it was only one time." My shoulders slump in disappointment. His eyes search mine as if he's remembering. "Hey wait, look at me." he forces my eyes back to his, and for the first time in months I'm met with longing and need. The way his eyes shine makes my heart lurch in my chest. How can my body and heart be so forgiving while my brain is still a few steps behind? "We'll figure it out…together." He promises. A stray tear slides down my cheek and he swipes it away with his thumb.

"How?" I manage to squeak out. "You hurt me so bad Gideon." I confess. When everything happened my heart literally shattered into a million pieces. I've spent the last five months slowly putting it back together again. I cover my face with my hands, not wanting to show him the pain he caused me, the pain he still causes me.

"Not a day goes by that I don't regret what I did to you. I love you Snow. I've loved you since the first day I met you. I wanted you when I found you in my yard, craved you when I had you in my bed, loved you when I watched you run across the beach without a care in the world. I haven't stopped."

"I can't do it again Gideon." I sigh. My hand rests against my belly protectively. "It's not just me anymore, you broke my heart and I won't let you do that to my baby...to our baby." he swallows hard.

"I'll do whatever it takes." He says with conviction. I believe him, but it's going to take a hell of a lot more to trust him again.

"I don't know if that's enough." I sigh as I look away. With Gideon standing so close to me my entire body and mind is going haywire.

"I'll prove it to you. I'll show you it is." His thumb and forefinger grip my chin and force me to stare back into his dark pools of chocolate. "I'll spend the rest of my fucking life, proving it to you." His words are laced with heavy conviction. I stay there transfixed on the beautiful man before me. I manage to nod, and then wonder if he even saw it.

Chapter 31

Gideon

"What is this?" Snow asks as she hops into my truck. She actually let me attend one of her doctor's appointments. I've been asking for weeks, and it's been like pulling teeth with her. I think I've managed to somewhat convince her that I'm here for good.

It wasn't hard when I made the decision to pack up my shit and move down here. Who'd of thought I'd ever end up in the middle of nowhere Alabama? It was just the first step in operation get Snow back. I needed her in my life, and my unborn child. The minute I discovered she was carrying my child I felt like a changed man. As if anything that ever happened before that minute didn't matter.

The minute I heard the heartbeat burst through that monitor I damn near had a heart attack. An emotion I've never felt so clear before resonated all the way deep down into my bones...unconditional love. I thought I loved Snow more than anything in this world. I thought I could never love anything or anyone more than her, but the minute I heard that tiny heartbeat that love was surpassed.

"You know...pamphlets." I shrug as we pull out of the parking lot.

"Pamphlets?" she asks in surprise. "For what?" she shoves them on the dashboard, turning towards me.

"Me." I wait for her to laugh but when I look over. Her eyes are shining with unshed tears.

"But these are pregnancy pamphlets." She speaks as if I've completely lost my damn mind.

"Yeah I know, Snow. I know shit about pregnancies. What if you need something and I can't fucking help you because I have no clue how?" just thinking about it has my skin crawling and my mind going completely nuts. I need to be able to take care of her, of them. I need to make sure I know every fucking thing about this because as of right fucking now I have no clue. Some people say it comes naturally to them, parenting…but I don't think that's true at all. The more I study this shit the more I feel as if I know nothing.

"So you decided to take every pamphlet from Doctor Short's office?" she raises an inquisitive brow.

"Yeah, well I saw some things on those that google failed to tell me." her jaw literally hangs open. Is it really that much of a surprise?

"Gideon…" her hand comes to rest on my thigh. I watch out of the corner of my eye as a stray tear slides down her face. I bring my thumb up to wipe the tears away.

"Don't cry, Snow." my voice comes out hoarse. "I just want to be ready."

"It's not like we're sending a rocket up to space, Gideon. It's a baby." she half laughs. It's not just a baby though, it's my baby, our child.

Everything I read and research just seems like it isn't enough. When we were in the doctor's office, I felt as if I knew nothing. I was weeks, months even, behind on the lingo.

"I can't fuck this up...like I did to us." I mutter the last part, but I know she hears it anyway. Her small fingers squeeze my thigh just a little bit harder, sending an unspoken message deep down inside of me.

"You won't." two words. She spoke two words yet they give me the power and absolution I need to keep going.

For Snow I'd do anything. I'd fight, scratch, and claw my way to the end of this goddamn earth for her. Little by little she's starting to realize that. Little by little I tear her walls down more and more, each and every day. She's slowly beginning to trust me again. I was prepared when I first came down here to lose her forever, but what I wasn't counting on was the ounce of hope that still resonates from deep down inside her heart.

She tells me it's because of the letters I sent that her heart just couldn't give up on me. In the same breath she swears she's only in it for Max. That damn dog huddles just a little closer every time she kids around like that with a smug look nestled on his huge furry face.

Thinking back on the events that lead us to this road, I feel a tad bit grateful. I spent most days thinking about all of the 'what if' moments I was faced with in the past year. If I had never taken that case against her mother, would I have even met Snow? If things had never escalated the way they had, would we have even ended up here?

It's hard to say what moments in life make us who we are today. What moment in time was the deciding factor that determines how the rest of your life would be? For me there were so many revolving around the tiny woman nestled tightly against my side. Every touch, every whisper, every single smile practically knocked me on my ass from the very beginning. I know I'll never be the same.

We will never be the same.

Chapter 32

Adeline

Rumors. They follow you around wherever you go. They capture you, they break you, and they own you...Unless you own them. I've been a product of gossip since before I even left the womb. I was meant to fulfill the destiny the whole town thought I was sure to have. I was on the path to destruction long before I met him... Gideon Wellfleet.

The man who changed my destiny and showed me something more. He thought he'd ruin me, told me he would. What he didn't know was pain and destruction followed me everywhere. It was only a matter of time before it got to him too.

Snow

We were a disaster waiting to happen. Two souls plagued by rumors and gossip. The words that followed us around most of our lives threatened to pull us under and tear us apart at every twist and turn. But Gideon and I were resilient...we were resilient together.

Together we have overcome almost every obstacle that has come between us, even if those obstacles were us. Gideon is afraid of what the future seems to hold. He's afraid of his impending fatherhood. What he doesn't realize is that he'll be okay. All his research will come in second place as soon as he sets his sights on our baby. He won't need any of it.

He once thought loving someone was something you had to learn to do. He spent most of his time avoiding anything and anyone. But he was wrong about all of that. His love for me came naturally as was mine for him. It can never be broken and torn, only threatened and tested. I know deep down I never gave up on his love for me, and I never will. No matter how fast it seemed to happen, or how fast it all seemed to crash down around us.

Rumors. They follow you around wherever you go bringing nothing but pain and destruction. It took me a while to finally see it but mine brought me him...

Gideon Wellfleet.

The man who changed my destiny and showed me something more.

Acknowledgements

Steve- Thank you for constantly helping me with just about everything, the formatting, editing, and the cover art. I don't know how you're not annoyed with me yet lol. Your support will always keep me going.

My work bae's Janie, Peg, Terri, Aimee & Shar- I'll always be grateful for you guys. You sit there for hours on end listening to all my crazy ideas and still act surprised when I change my mind for the millionth time. The endless amounts of red bull and snacks also help.

Josh, Fluff & Emma- Thanks for letting me constantly send you polls on what things I should say/do and when to do them. I literally couldn't do it without my fab three.

About The Author

B.K. Leigh is from a small town in central Massachusetts. When not at her full time job she enjoys spending her time outdoors with her longtime boyfriend. Fishing, cliff jumping, and long spontaneous road trips are her absolute favorite. When not outside exploring you can find her inside face-timing her many nieces and nephews, or cooped up on her comfy sack with her nose buried in a book. She has since turned her love for reading into writing. She loves creating stories based on what she likes to read, and hopes her readers loves them just as much.

Made in the USA
Middletown, DE
17 July 2023

34770898R00156